JANE AND KENNEDY DANIELS MYSTERIES

VOLUME 1

DAISY LANDISH

Second Edition

Editing by Rachael Lammie
Cover by Daisy Landish

BEACHES AND TRAILS
PUBLISHING

MURDERED ON HALLOWEEN

A COZY MYSTERY

CHAPTER 1
A NIGHT OF TRICKS AND TREATS

FOR MOST, October 31st, aka Halloween, marks the start of the holiday season. It starts the countdown to Christmas and New Year's. Jane Daniels had always been a bit of a sleuth. She loved mysteries, crime novels, and drama. One of her favourite pastimes was curling up on the sofa with her wife, Kennedy, to watch serial killer documentaries while piecing everything together before the celebrity narrator revealed the killer. The fact that Kennedy enjoyed the same was one of the things that had first attracted Jane to her wife. Jane and Kennedy met in college while Kennedy was on an exchange program. It was love at first sight. They both loved mysteries, and Jane had a talent for solving crimes. Jane looked at mysteries as puzzles, seeing them as just missing that vital piece. And she needed to find it.

But she also loved a good bargain. She loved hunting around shops for that bargain item she could brag about. She considered every shopping expedition an excuse to hunt for treasure. The X on her mental treasure map always turned out to be the location of the most discounted item in the particular store she was in. Jane loved hunting thrift shops around Halloween. She would find missed and forgotten outfits and pieces that she could craft into the perfect Halloween costume. A piece that was one of a kind. And this year was no exception. The mayor had invited Jane and Kennedy to the big Halloween celebration. Jane was determined that this year's costumes would be better than ever.

Meanwhile, Kennedy was the cyber-wizard of the family. She loved it when Jane came home with a new gadget. She loved nothing more than to add something new to her electronics collection, especially something that she could use to make everyday life easier and more enjoyable. Kennedy had practically automated every inch of their home. It was like living in the future. Having a top-notch home meant they had more time to spend with each other, which helped them stay close as a couple.

Kennedy's favourite part of Halloween was creating a new, scary contraption to spook the trick or treaters with. At first, Jane thought it was cruel until she saw how much the children looked forward to seeing what would jump out at them this year.

Kennedy was a reasonably intelligent woman. She was very proud of her M.I.T. education. Her keen intellect was why Detective Inspector Arthur Gottfried often consulted her regarding some of his more complex crime cases. She had helped on several occasions that year alone, and even more since she had moved to the U.K. full time from her home in Boston, Massachusetts.

Jane and Kennedy had a lot in common, making their marriage strong, but they had other interests, which kept them from butting heads. Jane *loved* to bake. Something about baking was so relaxing and calming. And although Kennedy was a bit of an introvert, she managed to find her passion too. Coding gave her a sense of control and allowed her to explore the most that her mind had to offer. Their friends always admired the love they had for each other. As a result, their friends often referred to their successful marriage as *# couplegoals*.

For her part, Jane was a little jealous of the families that their friends were raising, wanting one of her own, but she never let it show. She was happy being 'fun aunty Jane' for the time being. Holidays and special occasions were her favourite time of year, and with Halloween fast approaching, her excitement grew.

She loved having all the children dressed up, knocking on her door and singing, "Trick or Treat!" Even Kennedy got involved with decorating the house. Kennedy took great pleasure in making the house as scary as possible, trying to outdo herself every year. For Jane, it was the chorus of laughter when the kids realised it was fake and the shrieks of glee when they were given fistfuls of candy that she loved most.

Jane would love nothing more than to have a child before her biological clock started to slow down. Lately, this had begun to be more of a pressing issue for Jane. Though on the surface, she'd accepted that this was not quite the right time for the Daniels family to have children. She buried herself in sleuthing and finding new gadgets to help them in their daily life and around the home, pretending that the ache to have a child would go away if she kept busy enough.

―――――

"OK, hon, here it is. The costumes to beat all costumes," Jane cheered, placing Kennedy's costume on the big armchair in the corner of the room.

Kennedy walked over and unpacked the costume with an eye roll and loving smirk. Brown pants with a tail attached, a matching jacket that, once fastened, completed a torso and a headpiece that could be worn covering the face or not. It didn't take much for Kennedy to piece the costume together. The large teal collar with the gold-plated tag gave the identity away. It was a Scooby-Doo costume!

"I know you said something simple, and you wanted a mask, but when I saw this, I thought it would be super cute. And if the trick or treaters knocked before we left for the party, they would love it too," Jane cheered, pulling her costume out of the bag and twirling around the room in "I used to love watching Scooby and the gang when I was little," she reminisced.

"I said I didn't want to be recognised. This is a full-blown disguise! I don't think my mother would recognise me in this," Kennedy exclaimed.

"Exactly, it's a costume ball. How often do we get invited to such things? We have to make the most of it," Jane chimed, trying on her matching mask over her eyes.

"I'll give you this. I love seeing how excited you get about these things," Kennedy smiled.

Kennedy wasn't much of a party person. She much preferred her wife's company and her few close friends. Hence, she wanted a mask; less chance of people stopping to talk if they didn't know who she was. But Kennedy often went to parties she didn't want to, purely to make Jane happy. Seeing Jane happy and excited always made the parties worthwhile. Even Kennedy had to admit that the mayor's ball was a once-in-a-lifetime event this year. So, she would be a fool to miss out.

———

"So, which member of the Scooby gang will you be?" Kennedy asked, sitting on the footstool, watching Jane play about with her ensemble and examining her outfit in more detail, still not fully understanding it. Her eyebrows were slightly furrowed, and the teal from the collar reflected off her blue eyes.

"Well, I thought couple's costumes would be fun. But I don't know if I can pull off Shaggy. So, I picked up a Shaggy costume and a Daphne costume. What do you think?" Jane smiled.

Kennedy grinned, "While I love the idea of us going as Shaggy and Scooby, I do love you in purple." Jane didn't look much like Daphne, she had brown hair and wasn't quite as thin, but she would have pulled it off well.

"I love me in purple too. But if we are doing couples costumes and we already have Shaggy and Scooby, one of us will *have* to be Shaggy. How fun will it be to be completely unrecognisable for a night? It will be fun," Jane nodded enthusiastically.

"Flip for it? Heads Shaggy, tails Scooby?" Kennedy laughed, pulling a pound coin from her jeans pocket, hiding the laugh at Jane's expression. She put the coin back before flipping it. Kennedy knew that Jane wouldn't want to be Scooby. Even if she dressed as Shaggy, Jane would still find a way to add a touch of feminine glamour to the outfit. Kennedy burst out laughing.

"Don't worry, sweetie, you can be Shaggy," Kennedy smiled.

"You're not mad?" Jane asked.

"What would I be mad at? I think all of this is hilarious," Kennedy laughed.

"Why?"

"Here I thought we were going to a Halloween party dressed as ghosts with sheets over our heads. You know, simple."

Jane burst out laughing at Kennedy's crazy suggestion.

"Plus, even in a mask and being unrecognisable, I am still going with the prettiest woman in the room," Kennedy winked. She loved flirting with her wife. Even after all this time, Jane still blushed like a schoolgirl.

Kennedy was tall and slender with deep black skin and beautiful ringlets that rested just above her elbows. Jane wasn't exaggerating; her wife was a total catch, and she knew it.

This was no ordinary Halloween party. It was an exclusive Halloween ball hosted by the mayor. The town's most significant, brightest, and elite would be there. It was a chance to meet some new people, some influential people. Sheets with eye holes would not cut it. While the primary goal of the evening was to have fun and relax, Kennedy was looking forward to making some new connections and treating the party as a networking event, much to Jane's annoyance.

———

The party in question was to be held at one of the most famous hotels in London – The Mandarin.

The Mandarin was known for being the place for celebrities and world royals. It was a hotel steeped in history, extravagance, and luxury. Every day, it was crowded with fans hoping to catch a glimpse of their favourite pop star or movie star, sporting heroes, or just to glimpse how the other half lived.

The mayor herself was hosting, Mayor Clara Porter. It was to be a night to relax and have fun. The mayor had only invited the most influential people in the city to join in the night's festivities. Kennedy and Jane thought it was odd that the party was so exclusive but theorised that the mayor created an opportunity to meet her favourite celebrities and didn't want other folks to get in her way.

Rumour had it that there was to be a live band, someone pretty famous, performing for the night. The guest list had been kept strictly confidential. It was the talk of London who would be going to such a party.

Jane had assumed that the only reason she and Kennedy had been invited was because of Kennedy's ongoing help with Detective Arthur Gottfried. Kennedy worked as a freelance programmer, and occasionally Detective Gottfried needed help with working on new technology for his office or, more likely, to gather information about their latest suspect. Throughout their working relationship, the girls and Arthur had bonded and considered themselves close friends.

No matter the reason for the invite, Jane was excited to go. Kennedy's invitation was ambiguous and didn't directly state whether Jane was invited to the event, but Jane was sure Kennedy would get crafty if they ran into any problems. The invitation said the theme of the party was "Halloween Horrors." It was exciting to think about the decorations that would be inside. Even though Kennedy usually made Halloween decorations, seeing some at the event would still be fun.

However, she did feel slightly disappointed at missing out on the trick-or-treating fun with the neighbourhood kids this year. When the kids found out that there would be no haunted house decorating the front yard and no spooky traps jumping out at them, they were disappointed. But when Jane promised that she would get autographs if any of their favourite celebrities attended, the kids soon perked up again.

Every reporter, social media influencer, and gossip rag had followed Mayor Porter around for the last two months while she organised the event, hunting like vultures for any minute detail they could publish. Eventually, Mayor Porter decided to give them a little taste of the evening.

"The bar shall only be servicing beer and wine and will close at 11 p.m. I don't want anyone driving home drunk. Taxis will be supplied for everyone and anyone over the limit. That will be all," Mayor Porter announced.

The small gathering of reporters grunted with disappointment. They had hoped for something juicy to get the readers flipping the pages or subscribers watching videos. But Mayor Porter was known for keeping her cards close to her chest. So, all that anyone outside of a strict handful of people knew was the location, the date, that it was a costume ball, and now that the bar would close at eleven.

"Come on, Mayor Porter! Just one name! An industry even. Will there be athletes there? Movie stars?" begged the paparazzi.

"I can neither confirm nor deny," Mayor Porter grinned, taking great pleasure in making the media squirm.

CHAPTER 2
COSTUMES AND CHAOS

THE TAXI PULLED up outside The Mandarin, leaving Jane and Kennedy to gasp and awe at the decorations. Police lined the streets holding back fans hoping to spot celebrities and paparazzi hoping to catch a snap of the guests. A long red carpet lined the pavement from the drop-off point to the large golden double doors. Performers dressed as ghouls danced with fire while others showed off their fire-breathing skills, keeping everyone outside entertained. Lights leapt across the sky above the hotel. Goosebumps pricked Jane and Kennedy's skin. They knew that tonight would be a night they would never forget.

Stepping out of the taxi, the pair were relieved to have opted for costumes involving masks. It gave them a sense of privacy that they imagined the celebrity guests didn't get too often. Blinding flashes of lights erupted around them as the paparazzi made every effort to capture their picture.

"I kind of feel like a celebrity myself," Jane grinned.

"Let's give them a show, shall we? Enjoy our fifteen seconds of fame?" Kennedy chuckled.

"Look! Over there! Who are you?" yelled one paparazzi as he flashed his camera.

"Take off the mask!" yelled another.

They gave the crowd a quick wave, striking a few poses and hearing them scream their approval. Blinking back the blinding lights of hundreds of cameras, Jane and Kennedy chuckled as they headed to the door.

A tall, distinguished gentleman in a royal blue suit, hat, and white gloves with a gold chain attached to his pocket watch smiled at them as they approached. Kennedy was surprised that the doorman wasn't in fancy dress, considering everyone else in and around the building was. Even the security team wore Halloween costumes, which Jane found very amusing. She imagined the big beefy security guard, who was dressed as a clown, chasing someone down the street, stifling a laugh as the thought took over her mind.

"Good evening, do you have an invitation?" he asked with a slight bow of his head.

"Yes, here you go," Jane smiled, pulling the invitation from her purse.

One quick look over, he nodded and opened the door.

"Head left at the sign and follow the arrows to the grand ballroom. Enjoy your evening, Mrs and Mrs Daniels."

"Thank you," Kennedy smiled back, offering her hand to shake.

The doorman winked and smiled back, quietly placing the tip that Kennedy had slid him into his pants pocket. She had seen the move done several times in movies, but her favourite was in her guilty pleasure – F.R.I.E.N.D.S. reruns. She had been waiting so long for an opportunity to try it. It was fun to get a taste of how the rich and famous live.

———

When Jane and Kennedy reached the ballroom, they were amazed that it spanned two floors. A large spiral staircase separated the two, with black, purple, and orange decorations. A large chandelier hung from the ceiling, and a small gathering of guests dressed in an array of ornate costumes donned the dance floor below. A band was set up and playing from the main stage; they were all dressed in costume. Jane had been looking forward to seeing who the mystery band performing would be, but their costumes concealed their identities. Jane looked forward to figuring out who the singers were all evening.

Jane and Kennedy stood at the top of the staircase, admiring the room. The door closing behind them alerted the other guests to their arrival; all eyes in the room drifted up to them, watching with beaming smiles as they descended the staircase of the far wall of the dance floor.

The room was like nothing either of them had seen before. Surrounding the dance floor sat rows of tables filled with couples who were not ready to start dancing yet. As they drew further down the stairs, the decorations came into view. The mayor had worked her magic. The room was decorated like a haunted house. Pedestals scattered the room with performers dressed as ghouls and ghosts., jumping out at guests who got too close. Each performer twirled ribbons, buttons, or hoops, giving the guests a show like no other. Small glass cages scattered across the bar area filled with snakes and spiders. Kennedy hoped they were fake as she wasn't too fond of snakes, nor Jane of spiders. It wasn't until later that evening that they found out the local zoo had loaned the creatures out for the evening.

"This is incredible," Jane whispered to Kennedy.

"It's like entering another world," Jane awed.

"I know, Mayor Porter has impressed me," Kennedy admitted.

Kennedy may have been reluctant to go to the party at first. But now that she was there, she found she was looking forward to the rest of the evening and was glad that Jane had insisted on them going. Kennedy admired the animatronics that flew around the room as the tech geek she was. Small drones were operating mechanical witches, ghouls, and ghosts. There really was something for everyone there that evening.

———

As soon as they reached the bottom step, they were immediately greeted by a stranger dressed as Fred from the Scooby gang. Whoever he was appeared to have been waiting for them, tucked in the shadows of the stairs. He jumped out with such enthusiasm that both Kennedy and Jane jumped, startled before chuckling to themselves.

"You guys look amazing," he laughed heartily.

"Arthur, you look incredible. All we need now is a Daphne and Velma. We have the entire Scooby gang," Jane laughed, admiring how well Arthur pulled off the ascot and blonde wig.

"Great minds shop alike," Arthur beamed, showing off his costume. He was obviously very proud of his effort. "Scooby and Shaggy, a great combination. You both look fantastic."

Jane giggled back happily while Kennedy offered a proud bow. But, of course, Arthur would see right through their disguises. He was a phenomenal detective, after all.

"This venue is incredible; it must be costing the city a mint to host such an extravagant ball," Kennedy said, stepping aside as more guests descended the stairs.

"Nah, everyone has chipped in. The fire department, the police, and other emergency services. We helped decorate and even paid for some of the snacks and cocktails. It's nothing fancy, but we felt we should do our part," Arthur replied.

Jane and Kennedy nodded back, their eyes dancing around the room, admiring the show.

"Madame Mayor has done us proud. We are all here to have fun. So come on, let's have some fun," Arthur laughed, heading off into the crowd.

It wasn't long before Jane and Kennedy lost Arthur in the crowd, but they had no doubt they would see him again as the night drew on.

———

An hour later, the party was in full swing. The dance floor was full of dancing couples. A small selection of paparazzi had been let inside, closely monitored by the Mayor's P.R. team.

Many of the officers had invited friends to join the fun. Everyone had made an extra effort to disguise themselves—guests dressed as pirates, ghosts, vampires, and zombies.

The room was a mix of characters. While the Daniels' admired the

Halloween-themed costumes, Jane loved the extravagance of some of the more elaborate and glamorous outfits. There was a Cleopatra donned in heaps of gold and turquoise jewellery. A Mary Queen of Scots, a Joan of Arc, Greek goddesses, and movie stars. Even Mayor Clara Porter looked stunning, dressed as Marie Antoinette.

The selection was truly unique. There was even another Scooby-Doo in the same costume. The only difference between Kennedy and the other Scooby-Doo was the shoes. Kennedy wore red Sabot-like shoes, pointed at the toe with a red leather-pressed bow and gold short metal studs, with a small heel so she could feel a little feminine in the dog costume. The gentleman who wore the same outfit had opted for emerald-green velvet slippers.

I wish I had opted for slippers, Kennedy pondered.

Kennedy rarely wore high heels. While she was steady on her feet, she much preferred an excellent pair of comfortable flat shoes. Despite the short kitten-like heel on her shoes, her feet ached as she danced the night away with her wife.

CHAPTER 3
MURDER UNMASKED

TWO HOURS LATER, the evening was still going strong. Everyone was having the night of fun, relaxation, and networking that the mayor had planned. The night was proving to be a huge success. The band played *I Put a Spell on You*, *The Monster Mash*, and other Halloween-themed songs between more upbeat tunes, giving the guests a night to remember. Jane thought it was even more fun when songs like *Thriller* were played, and everyone joined in dancing in unison.

Jane and Kennedy danced the night away, and Kennedy made some new friends in the tech industry. Jane played off that she was annoyed Kennedy had brought her business cards. Secretly, she was proud that she had taken the initiative.

"I know I wasn't overly excited about tonight, but I'm happy you made me come," Kennedy smiled, kissing Jane softly on the forehead.

"See, I told you it would be fun. I'm just nipping to the ladies' room. Meet you at the bar when I get back?"

"Sure. Strawberry wine?" Kennedy replied.

Jane nodded back as she headed across the floor.

Jane headed to the ladies' room to freshen up her makeup and fix her hair. She smiled at her reflection and gave her wig a slight fluff up, and reapplied her makeup, beard, and eyeliner. She was preparing to head back to the party when she heard a woman's distressed scream coming from outside. Jane's heart pounded, her gut telling her something was amiss. The screams were not just those of a guest frightened by the night's festivities. Her inner voice told her to stay in the bathroom. But her heart ruled her head, and she followed the screams.

On the floor outside the men's bathroom, Jane saw a sight that stopped her heart cold. Panic, pain, and heartbreak ran through her as she looked at the Scooby-Doo lying on the floor with a bloodied hole staining the teal dog collar. A woman dressed as Velma cradled the body, covered in blood. The mask was untouched and perfect. The painted eyes looked even more haunting now that the life behind them was gone.

Tears streamed from Jane's eyes as she launched herself at the body on the floor, clawing at the jacket collar.

"Kennedy? Kennedy, what happened?" Jane cried.

"Kennedy? Why do you keep calling my husband that?" the woman cradling the body and shot her an icy look, her voice laced with pain and anger as confusion filled her eyes.

Jane stood, staring down at the body. Scanning, she noticed the green velvet slippers. The body wasn't Kennedy. Jane was suddenly racked with guilt. She felt relieved that the body lying dead on the floor wasn't her wife. She felt awful for feeling that way, even though she knew it was a normal human reaction. Her heart went out to the woman rocking back and forth, holding her husband.

"I'm so sorry…. you are right; that's not my wife. I'm so very, very sorry," Jane sobbed.

She scanned the crowd that flocked towards the commotion, hoping to see Kennedy and ease her pounding heart.

———

A small crowd of guests had gathered around the body, everyone curious about what had happened. Most thought it was all part of the evening—a show or a murder mystery, in fact. Shock quickly spread when realisation sunk in, and everyone was forced to admit someone had been murdered at the party. All too shocked and concerned to pull themselves away from the horror.

"Hold it, folks," boomed Arthur Gottfried's voice.

He pushed through the crowd, pulling off his ascot and wig and discarding them on a nearby table, instantly shifting from party mode to detective mode.

"This is now an active crime scene. Many of you know what that means," Arthur said, pushing the crowd back as several other officers rushed forward, surrounding the scene with yellow crime scene tape.

"Only the M.E. and assigned officers are allowed past the yellow tape. So now everyone, please step back," Detective Gottfried boomed.

The guests knew what that meant. Many of them would be questioned and asked to go to the precinct to give a statement. Everyone at the party was now a suspect. The ballroom was locked down. No one was allowed to leave, and no one was allowed to enter until the scene had been examined.

Meanwhile, Madame Mayor was none too pleased, "Who is this man?" she asked Detective Gottfried.

"My husband, Judge Rainford," sniffled the dead man's wife.

"My condolences, Mrs Rainford. Please, follow me. Let's get you away from the crowd. Arthur, can I take her up to my suite?" the mayor asked.

"I will assign officers to accompany you," Arthur nodded.

Even the mayor was a suspect until proven otherwise. Arthur was reluctant to let her or the wife leave, assigning several officers to guard the mayor's suite, ensuring that they didn't make a run for it or become the next target.

————

As the judge's identity flew around the room on the crowd's whispers, speculation floated closely behind. Everyone assumed that the judge had been targeted because of his unflinching attitude towards prosecuting criminals and gang members. He had judged many high-profile cases that year alone, never mind the rest of his twenty-year career.

Everyone sat, frustrated, scared, and agitated—a wonderful night ending in horror. The theme of the night, Halloween horrors, had come to pass. Fitting yet, ironic.

As rumours circled the room, Jane's mind began to wander, and fear gripped her heart. Her mind raced back to the recent incident with Kennedy's car. The brakes had failed, and after inspection, they found they had been tampered with.

What if Kennedy was the intended target? What would have happened if the judge had not been wearing the same costume? Could the two events be related? Jane panicked.

Kennedy hadn't seemed to make the connection; she had removed her headpiece and mask and undone her jacket and collar, giving herself a little more space to breathe, given the tense situation.

"That costume was way hotter than I thought it would be," Kennedy complained, fanning herself with a drink menu from one of the tables.

Seeing Kennedy so calm settled Jane's mind a little; perhaps she was overthinking things, but she still couldn't help but worry, and she didn't want to worry Kennedy until she had more evidence.

The police gathered statements and CCTV footage from the hotel, staff, and guests. Then, as more and more suspects were cleared of any suspicion, the police began allowing people to leave. To most, the cause of death seemed obvious. But the medical examiner was confused about where the shot had come from. A bullet to the neck seemed straightforward, but not to Dr Albertson, who had been with the twelfth precinct for some eleven years.

"You see, Lieutenant," Dr Albertson began. "If the victim had been shot at close range, there would be burn marks around the wound even with a silencer. But instead, the bullet went right through, and it's a particular bullet from the recovered shell."

Lieutenant Gilbert Evans stood waiting, listening intently to what the M.E. had to say.

"It's not your typical handheld calibre. It looks more like it came from a rifle. I will know more for sure once I get the results back from the lab. This does, however, mean that the shooter was at a distance and above the victim. I believe the forensic teams need to investigate the Juliette balcony and the Mezzanine landing above the stairs. Hopefully, the shooter left some evidence behind."

If the shooter was on the stair landing or the Juliette balcony, how had nobody seen them? An amateur would be caught in no time. And an amateur couldn't have made a shot so accurate from so far away.

"Thank you, doctor; I will get the team right on it. It's going to be a long night," Evans sighed, his mind racing.

Is this shooter a professional? Arthur shook his head, pulled out a notepad, and began to scribble down his thoughts.

CHAPTER 4
TARGETED FOR TERROR

THE NIGHT HAD BEEN long and tiresome. Detective Gottfried and Lieutenant Evans had left the party and headed straight to the precinct to begin their investigation. Lieutenant Evans had his suspicions, believing the bullet was a .22 calibre, but until he had spoken to the forensic team and had the report from the M.E., nothing was certain. He began to build a list of suspects: people from the party and people related to some of the judges' open cases. He was trying to create a map of connections, hoping he could find the common denominator to lead him to the shooter. The corkboard on his wall had photos of the party's attendees pinned to it, with strings connecting each photo to another.

"The C.S.I. teams are examining the upper floor this morning; I will let you know what they find as soon as I speak with them. Thank you, doctor. In the meantime, if you could give me the confirmation on the calibre of the bullet as soon as you can, I would appreciate it," Evans said, standing from the table in the medical examiner's office.

"I will send you my report as soon as I have it – Thanks for the coffee. It's exactly what I need after a sleepless night," Albertson yawned, leaving the room.

Later that afternoon, Evans was sitting in his office reviewing all the evidence that had been gathered. In such a short amount of time, it was impressive. Either his teams worked super hard, or the killer was sloppy. He smiled over the report; he had indeed been correct. The calibre of the bullet was a .22. This would prove to be a vital piece of evidence. The U.K. didn't have many guns, and even the forces were limited in their supply. Very few people had the expertise to control a weapon of such a calibre.

"This will make the list of suspects even smaller. We'll have this guy in no time," Evans smiled.

Evans often talked to himself in his office. He felt it helped him think clearer.

———

Meanwhile, back at the Daniels household, Jane had not been able to shake her feelings from the night before. She tried to tell herself that she was still in shock after the evening's events, which were now circulating on every news outlet and social media page. It felt suffocating. She wanted so badly to forget the judge's image dead on the floor. She tried to forget, even more, the pain in her chest when she thought it was Kennedy. Even thinking about it brought her back to tears. It seemed there would be no escape from the Halloween Horrors Ball.

With each news report, with details misinterpreted, Jane had more things to worry about. She still hadn't voiced her concerns to Kennedy. Pacing the kitchen, she did what she usually did when her mind spiralled. Pulling baking trays, cookie cutters, utensils, and mixing bowls from the kitchen cabinets, she began to remove ingredients from the fridge.

Baking always seemed to relax her. Her mind was so concentrated on measuring ingredients that there was no space left to worry. Without realising how much noise she was making, the slamming of tins on the counters brought Kennedy into the room.

She wrapped her arms around Jane's waist and kissed her wife softly on the cheek. She knew all too well that something was wrong when Jane became this chaotic.

"OK, sweetie, what's going on in that little head of yours? Are you hinting at new cake tins for Christmas?" Kennedy joked.

Jane spun around, looking lovingly up into Kennedy's eyes, her heart breaking at the thought that her concerns might have grounds.

"I think someone is trying to kill you," Jane choked.

Kennedy shrugged off the comment to Jane's horror, letting Jane go, and headed to the fridge to collect a fizzy drink. Little did Jane know, a similar thought had already crossed Kennedy's mind. But what sense would it make to worry her more?

"Don't do that, Jane. I know what you're thinking, and conjecture of this kind often leads to nothing. The judge and I wore the same costume – granted, but that means nothing. So why would I be a target?" Kennedy said, trying to soothe her wife.

———

Kennedy headed back to her home office. She wanted to get back to the new tech venture she was working on, thanks to the connections she made last night before all hell had broken loose.

"What about the brakes? They had been tampered with. Do you think that is a coincidence?" Jane insisted, following Kennedy inside, maintaining her stance.

With her querying gaze, Jane wanted Kennedy not to dismiss her concerns so lightly.

"Maybe, maybe not," Kennedy shrugged again.

"How can you dismiss this so easily?" Jane asked, alarmed.

"Look, when I took the car for its M.O.T., I picked it up from the garage after leaving a note for Charlie to send me the bill. The brakes were already marked as a concern, and Charlie had suggested I get them looked at as soon as possible. I planned to book them in after meeting with the guys from the tech convention a few days later. I simply forgot," Kennedy tried to reassure Jane, but nothing she said eased Jane's mind. "Purely coincidental."

Jane noted how Kennedy refused to meet her eye; Kennedy's gaze was planted on the floor. Jane knew that while Kennedy believed everything she said, she was still a little worried.

"I appreciate your concern, and I love you. I'm sure no one is after me. Whoever shot the judge will be apprehended soon enough. That will allay all your silly fears," Kennedy turned away, sitting at her desk and typing away, indicating the discussion was over.

Jane watched Kennedy for a few minutes before scoffing in frustration and noisily heading back to the kitchen to bake as loudly as possible.

———

Jane's concerns were not as ungrounded as Kennedy would have liked. Four days later, the police were no closer to apprehending the suspect. They had almost run out of leads and were drawing close to labelling it as a cold case.

Kennedy had headed out to a meeting with MedTech, a new medical technology company working on advanced medical equipment to aid in the recovery of injured soldiers in the field. The meeting was scheduled for two-thirty that afternoon in Kent. Kennedy was trying to be brave for Jane's sake, but after her outburst days before, Kennedy had made excuses not to use the car. So instead, Kennedy headed to the London Underground to catch her train.

Subconsciously, Kennedy walked through the streets of London with one eye constantly looking over her shoulder. Not watching where she was going, she almost walked into a mother and her baby coming up from the Underground.

"I'm so sorry, I wasn't watching where I was going," she apologised.

"It's OK. No one was hurt," smiled back the mother.

I'm paranoid, letting Jane's groundless concerns cloud my judgement, Kennedy thought, heading down past the turnstiles on the platform.

Her train was delayed. Pacing the platform to keep herself warm, Kennedy stopped, her heart pounding. A man stood in an alcove in a dark hooded leather jacket concealing most of his face. Usually, Kennedy would think nothing of it, but she had seen that figure before, following her from close to home. She had even seen him when she almost bumped into the mother just moments before.

Is he following me? Kennedy asked herself, trying to convince herself she was being paranoid.

Changing her path, moving between the crowd, she kept a close eye. Sure enough, the man followed. When Kennedy boarded her train, she lost sight of him. Looking through the train window, she was convinced she saw him still on the platform. Taking a breath, she sighed in frustration. *Purely paranoia.*

Listening to her music and scanning her notes for the rest of the journey, Kennedy allowed herself to relax, and excitement grew for her meeting. MedTech was using artificial intelligence and data science to reduce the number of misdiagnosed patients all around the globe. It was brilliant and would save the healthcare industry millions of pounds each year. Most importantly, it could help improve the quality of care for an unlimited number of patients. They were pushing for those funds to be rerouted into nurses' salaries.

She began to zone out, thinking about how incredible technology was. Closing her eyes, she leaned back and thought about how much life would improve over the next few decades. With A.I., the possibilities seemed endless.

Kennedy opened her eyes and was face to face with another mother and her twin babies. Her heart swelled, and she smiled. She realised that she wanted to have a baby, too. Kennedy had considered it before, of course, but hadn't seriously considered it until today. She shook her head and decided that she would talk to Jane after things had calmed down for them.

Her stop was nearing, and she was cutting it close to arriving at her meeting on time. She thought she had left early enough.

The figure she had seen at the first station reappeared as she packed her belongings into her bag and prepared to dismount at the next station.

Instinct kicked in, and she ducked out of the way. The blade missed her chest but sliced through her arm. Pain shot through her, and she cried out as blood began to pour down, soaking the floor as her heart beat faster in fear.

The train doors opened, and the figure took off. Kennedy ran down the platform after him, adrenaline pumping, holding tight to the gash in her arm, trying her best to control the bleeding. But unfortunately, the figure was too far ahead. He ran with the performance of a track runner, launching himself up the stairs, taking them two at a time.

"Hey, stop!" yelled a policeman who had followed Kennedy off the train, his partner charging passed, catching up on the figure as the two disappeared from sight.

"My partner has it covered. Let's get you to sit down and look at that wound," the policeman said, taking hold of Kennedy and leading her to a bench by the wall.

Sitting down, Kennedy took several slow, deep breaths to calm the adrenaline that flowed through her, making her tremble. *What was going on? What was happening?* Kennedy was confused, frustrated, and angry all at once.

"Now, why don't you tell me your name and what happened?" asked the policeman after he called on his radio for assistance.

CHAPTER 5
A HACKER'S WEB

IT TOOK ROUGHLY HALF an hour for the ambulance to get across the busy London streets in the afternoon. With rush hour traffic, Kennedy was honestly surprised it hadn't taken longer. Kennedy sat in the ambulance, contemplating what had happened after the E.M.T. had cleaned up her arm and bandaged her. Thanks to her quick reflexes, the wound wasn't as bad as it could have been. Only a handful of stitches were required; the muscle wasn't too severely damaged as the blade hadn't plunged too deep, and Kennedy didn't even need to go to the E.R. to get it sorted.

Once the E.M.T. had given her the all-clear, Kennedy sat and told the police officer everything that happened. She ran over the details of all the places she had seen him and realised that she had noticed him following her for a while. She also thought it best to inform him of Jane's concerns and how the incident could be linked to the murdered judge.

"I'm sorry to have to tell you this, Mrs Daniels, but we lost the suspect," Officer Lancaster said, joining his colleague in the ambulance.

Kennedy smiled back at him weakly and thanked him for his effort, even as her heart began to race at the thought of him still being out there, able to get to her, or worse, Jane.

"If you could please describe the man as best as you can to the sketch artist, we will get a BOLO out of him before the day is out," the officer said, introducing the criminal sketch artist.

Kennedy was furious and in no mood to discuss the matter any further. She was scared and angry, not just at the perp but at herself. She shouldn't have ignored Jane's concerns. Jane had been right. She should have called Arthur and voiced her concerns sooner; perhaps all this mess could have been avoided. Kennedy had no idea why she had questioned Jane's concerns. She had a knack for these things and was never wrong.

Closing her eyes, trying to calm her mind and temper, Kennedy remembered something. Something that could lead to the arrest of such a lunatic. The man who attacked her, they had met before, online. He had tried to contact her several weeks back. He wanted Kennedy's help to hack the police network.

"Just for fun," he had said.

None of this was what Kennedy would class as fun.

"His name is Devon," Kennedy realised.

———

Kennedy couldn't understand how the situation had gotten so out of hand. How had a simple 'no' turned into a vengeful act that had resulted in the murder of a judge and an attack on her?

"This man is crazy, officer," Kennedy said.

"So, you know him?" asked the officer.

"Not officially. I met him online. He is a first-rate hacker, one of the best I have ever seen. When he asked me to hack the police network, I turned him down and was alerted to his presence again when Detective Inspector Gottfried alerted me to the police network being hacked," Kennedy replied.

"I remember that hacking," the other officer gasped, "we couldn't get back in for days. They had to call some tech wiz to get us back into the network."

"That was me," Kennedy smiled, a hint of pride shooting through her that her reputation proceeded her. "This guy is a wizard at covering his tracks online. I couldn't track him, but I managed to kick him out and block him from re-accessing the network. I only met him in person once before, but I can give you a detailed description," Kennedy answered.

Satisfied that everything had been taken care of at the train station, Kennedy accompanied the officers to their vehicle, mindlessly watching the hustle and bustle of London pass her by from the car window.

————

Kennedy accompanied the officers back to the station. She finished her description with the sketch artist and filed her statement. Several hours later, feeling calmer but mentally exhausted, Kennedy returned home to find Jane up in arms. As expected, Detective Arthur Gottfried notified Jane of what had occurred.

"What on earth were you doing on the Underground? We have two cars, for crying out loud!" Jane yelled.

"I was taking your suggestion," she laughed nervously, trying to make light of the situation. "My car is booked in next week to get the brakes fixed, and I thought you might need your car today."

"Are you serious? You could have been killed!" Jane yelled, shaking her head in frustration.

Pausing, Jane sighed heavily, launching herself at Kennedy and pulling her into a hug. She never wanted to let her wife out of her sight again. The thought of losing her once was bad enough but twice was almost too much to bear. Kennedy could feel Jane trembling as she gripped her tighter.

"I was so worried," Jane whispered, holding back tears.

Kennedy hugged her wife, comforting her, her heart filled with love for Jane.

"I know, but I'm OK now," Kennedy reassured, taking Jane's face in her hands and staring lovingly into her eyes.

"Arthur is coming over for dinner. He called before you arrived.

They found the guy's flat; it was empty, his computers gone. He has run," Jane said.

Kennedy nodded, shrugging off her jacket and hanging it on the coat rack by the front door.

"I figured as much, but I'm sure I can find him online," Kennedy headed to the kitchen to make herself a much-needed coffee. Being from Boston, she didn't quite understand why everyone in London seemingly loved tea. Kennedy was essentially indifferent to it. She figured that her influence had rubbed off on Jane and Arthur, though, because they nearly always drank coffee.

"What do you mean?"

"Guys like him can't stay offline without logging in somewhere. And when he does, I will find him," Kennedy answered.

Tea in hand, Kennedy turned on her computer with a newfound determination to find her attacker. He had managed to evade her once; she was determined it wouldn't happen again.

———

It was becoming a bit of a theme; whenever Arthur needed advice about a case, he would always find his way over around dinner time. In all honesty, Kennedy couldn't blame him. Jane was a fantastic cook, as well as a baker. Arthur had made no effort to let them know how much he preferred Jane's cakes to his wife's. A secret he made them both promise to keep.

"And you think this hacker is the same guy who shot the judge?" Arthur asked, blotting his mouth with his napkin.

Jane began to clear the table after their meal, leaving Kennedy to discuss her thoughts with the detective.

"I don't know enough about him to answer that question, Arthur," Kennedy answered. "All I know is he served in Afghanistan and came home two years ago. He said to avoid the nightmares and other symptoms of his P.T.S.D., he went into computer gaming as a distraction."

Arthur nodded, taking it all in, stirring his coffee pensively, "Did he happen to mention what regiment he belonged to?"

"No," Kennedy shook her head. "But I'm guessing if it was a sniper unit, it would make sense that he was the one to shoot the judge."

"I don't know much about specialised units in the army, but I doubt there are many that require both an expert hacker and a sniper. Was he in active combat? Do you think he was an army tech who happened to see some things he wasn't supposed to?" Jane said as she filled their cups with more coffee.

"No, he was definitely in active combat. He went into graphic detail about how he had seen his men gunned down. It was quite alarming," Kennedy admitted.

Jane shot Kennedy a look. *Why didn't she tell me about this?* She felt a pang in her chest. *I trust Kennedy, but I always thought we were honest with each other. She's never kept something this important from me.*

The room fell into an awkward silence. Whoever this man was, he was obviously troubled, skilled, and highly dangerous.

"Do you think he could be coming after Kennedy simply because he knows she knows who he is and can lead the police to him?" Jane asked.

"It's a genuine possibility. No one knows who he is apart from Kennedy. But, on the other hand, he could be trying to tie up any loose ends," Arthur pondered, instantly regretting his choice of words by the concerned looks on both Jane and Kennedy's faces.

CHAPTER 6
A HALLOWEEN TO REMEMBER

ON THE ADVICE of the police services, Jane and Kennedy locked themselves away at home until the shooter was apprehended. To keep herself occupied, Kennedy searched online for any trace of him, any scrap of information that could aid in his capture. To her surprise, her proactive approach eased Jane's mind. Jane wasn't coping very well with being locked indoors; she missed her job and her routine. She was happy to have time to spend with Kennedy, though.

They spent the long days cuddling on the couch watching boring daytime T.V. and were on track to gain a stone each from eating all the baked goods that resulted from Jane's stress.

After several days of searching, Kennedy had found nothing. He hadn't been online since before the judge's shooting. That doesn't mean Kennedy left empty-handed, thanks to having the last known location of his apartment; thanks to Detective Gottfried, she had his last known I.P. address. With that, she found every Wi-Fi tower his I.P. address had pinged off of over the previous year. She found several locations where he had spent long periods of time, and she handed this over to the police in hopes it would aid them.

Internet cafés, libraries, and other apartment buildings. All very different locations scattered across London. Each site had him logged in for hours. She managed to find a trail of what games he played, what forums he was a part of and all his social media. Some of his posts were alarming, but while Kennedy should have been scared, she felt for the young man. He was in pain, frightened, and alone in the world. He had fought for his country, and everyone had abandoned him.

With only meeting him once until that point, all Kennedy had was Devon's name. Now, she had everything. His full name was Devon Allen Maldin, and he was indeed a sniper in the fifth regiment. Before he joined the army, he had a promising future. He had been accepted to both Oxford and Cambridge and several prestigious universities overseas. His I.Q. was astounding; Kennedy wished she had met him under different circumstances. The things they could learn from each other, the ways they could change the world. The prospect of a future robbed from the world pained Kennedy.

He was a troubled young lad; his lack of medication to help his P.T.S.D. was shocking. And from what Kennedy had found, he hadn't filled his prescription in months or been to any of his scheduled therapy meetings. That said, no one had made any effort to check in on him. His doctors surely must have seen that his medications were not being collected, and his therapist must have noticed when he stopped showing up. So why had no one gone looking for him? Why had the police not been alerted that he was a missing person?

Seeing how troubled Devon Maldin was should have had Kennedy more concerned for her safety, but all it did was make her feel sorry for him. The more information Kennedy found on Devon, the more she wanted to find him. Not to have him arrested, but to help him. The world may have turned its back on Devon, but Kennedy wouldn't.

———

Almost a month had passed since Devon attacked Kennedy on the London Underground. Jane and Kennedy were starting to go a bit stair crazy being locked up in their home, flinching at every knock on the door, even when they had ordered food. The pair were both on edge. Around the clock, police surveillance was set up outside their house. It was meant for safety, but the home began to feel more like a prison after a while.

One morning while Jane baked yet another Victoria sponge cake – she had baked so much that Kennedy offered to buy her own bakery once all this Halloween drama was behind them. Kennedy sat at her computer researching P.T.S.D., local charities and organisations, and tech companies getting in on the ground floor with new technology to help recovering veterans with their condition. A gentle knock on the front door startled her.

"It's OK, sweetie; I know that knock. It's Arthur." Jane said, heading to the door to let in their friend.

"Good morning, Jane. Can I have a word with you and Kennedy?" Arthur asked, looking a little grim.

"Of course, head to the kitchen. I will make coffee. You are just in time; I just finished decorating a Victoria sponge cake," Jane smiled.

"My favourite."

"You always did have impeccable timing, Arthur," Kennedy grinned, joining them at the kitchen table.

Kennedy and Arthur made small talk waiting for Jane while she plated up the cake and brought over a fresh pot of coffee, a small pot of sugar cubes and two small jugs, one with milk and the other cream. The coffee smelled strong but not bitter. Jane made the best coffee. It never tasted too strong but wasn't weak, either—a perfect balance.

"So, Arthur, what brings you here so early in the morning?" Jane asked politely, subtly grabbing Kennedy's hand under the table.

"Devon Maldin? We found him," Arthur said before taking a bite of cake.

Kennedy and Jane let out a sigh of relief, releasing a breath they didn't realise they were holding.

"Where did you find him?" Jane asked.

Arthur looked up grimly, regret and sorrow swimming in his gaze. Then, dabbing the edges of his mouth with his napkin, he shook his head softly.

"After we put out the city-wide BOLO, we received a call from some kids in the park between here and the station where he attacked you. Looked like he had been living rough for a while, surviving on scraps found in the bins. It was.... rough," Arthur replied.

"Is he OK?" Kennedy asked, sorrow tugging at her heart.

"He will be, he is getting medical treatment right now, and the police are looking at a rehabilitation centre for P.T.S.D. sufferers," Arthur went quiet, fiddling with his napkin and making several attempts to ask a question he clearly didn't want to ask.

"Spit it out, Gottfried," Kennedy snapped.

"Right... With his current mental state, a judge has deemed him innocent on the grounds of mental incapacity in the judge's shooting. Understandable, due to his state of mind.... however, his attack on you seemed premeditated. I have to ask...do you wish to press charges?"

They shook their heads; they had gone over the pros and cons during their isolation and had decided it wasn't worth potentially ruining someone's opportunity to get help.

———

"Press charges? How could I? He needs help. Looking back now, I guess he was crying out for help, and I just didn't see it. How could I send that man to prison?" Kennedy asked, troubled.

Standing, she began to pace back and forth across the kitchen. She had vowed she wouldn't turn her back on him like everyone else. She knew that pressing charges wouldn't solve anything. It wouldn't help her sleep at night, and it wouldn't heal her scar or make Jane any less worried. All it would do would stress out an already deeply troubled soul.

"He did try to kill you, Kennedy. Even if he is in prison, I'm sure he will still get the help he needs, right Arthur?" Jane asked.

"Unfortunately, I can't answer that question," Arthur said regretfully. "I'm afraid the noises from prison, the violence we all know goes on behind closed doors yet choose to ignore; it could all act as triggers, and he could end up hurting someone else, or worse, or get himself killed."

"Can I see him? Can I talk to him?" Kennedy asked.

Jane jumped to her feet, alarmed, "You can't be serious?"

"Perhaps if I can speak with him, I could get answers."

"Honestly, Kennedy, what will that do? Will it help him or you?" Arthur asked.

Kennedy looked between her wife and her friend; neither of them understood what she needed. Finally, frustrated and confused, she headed to her office, slamming the door a little harder than intended before locking it tightly.

She spent the rest of the evening scrolling through all of Devon's social media, all of the medical records she could legally access, and any articles about his time in the army. She didn't want to believe a man who was willing to risk his life for the Queen and country could maliciously hurt anyone. Instead, she wanted to try and figure out where exactly the system failed him and what help he would need to get his life back.

Two days passed since they apprehended Devon, and Kennedy had made several attempts to try and see him but was advised against it by the police psychologist. Jane wasn't happy when Kennedy made her decision, but after talking it through, she understood. Kennedy decided that Devon was innocent and just wanted him to get the help he needed.

Kennedy didn't blame him; she didn't pity him either. Instead, she saw what happened as an opportunity for change.

––––––

"Morning sweetie, Arthur just called," Kennedy said, presenting Jane with her breakfast.

"How is he?"

"Good. Devon has been deemed unfit to stand trial. Kennedy answered that the judge thinks he will spend the rest of his days in a mental institution," Kennedy answered.

"Well... that's a sobering thought. But at least he will finally be getting the help he needs. This country has neglected its troop's mental health for far too long. Hopefully, something good comes out of this, and the authorities start to take note, so it doesn't happen again."

Kennedy nodded, not knowing what else to say. Then, heading to the small T.V. on the kitchen counter, she flicked on the news. Good Morning Britain had just finished, and the nine a.m. news was starting. The first report was about Devon.

The news reporter went on to inform the nation how Devon's P.T.S.D. had been left untreated and unmanaged, and as a result, he had spiralled into violent, vengeful outbursts. In addition, he was suffering from panic attacks that were so severe that his vengeance had no boundaries. He was an ill man who needed help.

"This incident has alerted us to the epidemic in this country. We need to pay more attention to our servicemen and women's mental health and safety. They risk their lives to free millions of people from tyranny; they deserve more than a handshake when they arrive home," said the P.T.S.D. charity advocate.

"I couldn't have said it better myself," Kennedy nodded at the screen.

As Kennedy looked around her futuristic, almost fully automated home, her mind wandered. How could technology prevent this from happening in the future? What tech could she help build to stop soldiers from seeing the horrors of war? To eliminate unnecessary loss of life? That's when she decided that would be her new tech venture.

"I kind of feel like this was meant to happen to me," Kennedy pondered.

"How do you mean?" Jane asked.

"I was meant to see the results of human error and use it to create something to help us in the future."

"I think that's wonderful, honey, that you can take something so positive out of a horrible situation. I'm proud of you."

———

Kennedy hadn't been able to get the news report out of her head for days. Even as Jane prepared for Christmas, which was usually a happy time of year, Kennedy felt she needed to do more. So finally, she decided to reach out to the spokesperson who spoke on Devon's behalf on the news.

She set up a meeting for the New Year. Working with the charity was going to be her new venture. She vowed never to miss the signs of someone needing help again. After speaking with Arthur, he agreed it was an excellent idea; it would be the closure she needed on the incident. And even though she was told, due to the attack, she wouldn't be allowed to work with Devon directly; she was still able to help him. Even in a small way.

"How is he doing?" Jane asked when Kennedy ended her call.

"Slowly but surely," Kennedy replied.

"Did they get any answers on why he shot the judge?"

Kennedy sighed; she knew that Jane wouldn't like the answer.

"He insisted he didn't shoot the judge. He became quite distraught at the thought of it. He said his target was the Scooby-Doo. He said he didn't want the talking dog to interfere with his plans. He even quoted the show, saying how he would have got away with it if it wasn't for the dog and meddling kids. Arthur spoke to some of his old comrades. None of them knew he was suffering, and it seems a harmless prank stayed with him and manifested in nightmares when he got home."

"That's awful," Jane said.

Kennedy waited patiently, knowing it wouldn't be long before Jane put the pieces together.

"Wait! So, his target was... Kennedy...it could have been you he killed!" Jane panicked, "Why did he go after you? Imagine if the judge hadn't been wearing the same costume."

"No point in speculating on what could have happened. It doesn't help anyone. Apparently, when I refused to help him hack the police network, it triggered the 'baffoon' trying to stop his fun," Kennedy shrugged.

"Don't do that," Jane said softly, wrapping her arms around her wife.

"Do what?"

"I know that look. You are blaming yourself. How could you have known this is what would happen?"

Kennedy nodded; she knew Jane was right. She had done some research online, concerned about how she was feeling. Psychologists called it survivor's guilt. Kennedy realised that now, she and Devon had much more in common than just being good with a computer.

"A hunted house, a man haunted by the ghosts of his past. A life lost. I bet Mayor Porter never intended for her Halloween Ball to be so...."

"Memorable? In the worst possible way."

"Exactly."

"Well, I think it's safe to say this Halloween was one to remember," Jane sighed.

"One I would rather forget; now, let us start looking forward to Christmas," Kennedy smiled.

———

The following day, Jane sat curled up in a ball on the sofa, wrapped in what Kennedy knew was Jane's thinking blanket. Like a comforter from her childhood, a blanket her great grandmother had made.

Kennedy peaked around the living room door watching with a smile on her face. Jane smiled, stirring her hot chocolate, another tell of hers that Jane had picked up on over the years.

"What are you thinking?" Kennedy asked, joining Jane on the sofa and wrapping her arms around her.

"I was thinking about the trick or treaters we missed....and all the other things we could have missed if things had ended differently...."

"Baby, I've told you not to worry...."

"Please let me finish," Jane interrupted softly, "I then started thinking about how you took something positive out of the horrors of the night. I've been thinking about something for a while now, and I wanted to discuss it with you."

Jane paused, and Kennedy could feel she was shaking, nervous. Kennedy kissed her head and stroked her hair, reassuring her she could talk to her about anything.

"It's OK, baby; talk to me."

"I think it's time we...."

"Have a baby?"

Jane sat up, surprised by Kennedy's response. It was as if she had read her mind.

"Yes," Jane stuttered.

"I've been thinking about it too. Even in the tiniest way, I guess facing death makes you re-evaluate what's important. While I love my job and helping Arthur, I found the part of Halloween I missed the most was the kids. It's something you have wanted for a while, and don't think I haven't noticed how you put your dreams aside for me. Now I think we are ready."

"So... we... are going to start looking into having a kid?" Jane grinned.

Kennedy smiled a nodded back.

"I love you so much," Jane breathed, tears causing her eyes to glisten like stars as she flung her arms around Kennedy.

"Even though we are closer to Christmas now, I feel like this all resulted from Halloween. What was it you said yesterday?"

"A Halloween to remember," Jane smiled.

"A Halloween to remember," Kennedy winked.

The End

ARRESTED ON BOXING DAY

A COZY MYSTERY

CHAPTER 1
A BARGAIN GONE WRONG

JANE DANIELS HAD ALWAYS BEEN a bit of a sleuth. She loved mysteries, crime novels, and drama. One of her favourite past times was to curl up on the sofa with her wife, Kennedy, watching serial killer documentaries and trying to piece everything together before the celebrity narrator revealed who the killer was. The fact that Kennedy enjoyed the same thing was one of the things that had first attracted Jane to her wife. They both loved mysteries, and Jane had a talent for solving crimes. Jane looked at mysteries as puzzles, seeing them as just missing that vital piece, and she needed to find it.

But she also loved a good bargain. She loved hunting around the shops for that bargain item she could brag about. She considered every shopping expedition an excuse to hunt for treasure. The X on her mental treasure map was always the location of the most discounted item in the particular store she was in. Jane loved the after-Christmas sales the most. All the must-have items, new gadgets, and things she could put aside for the following year were at the best possible discount price, making them a definite, *Yes, please*! It was a yearly tradition to check out what treasures she could find on Boxing Day. Most shoppers would still be in bed, stuffed from Christmas dinner from the day before, assuring her that she could avoid the crowds if she went early.

Meanwhile, Kennedy was the cyber-wizard of the family. She loved it when Jane came home with a new gadget. She loved nothing more than adding something new to her electronics collection, especially anything she could use to make everyday life easier and more enjoyable. Kennedy had practically automated every inch of their home. It was like living in the future, and they loved it.

Kennedy was a reasonably intelligent woman. She was very proud of her M.I.T. education. Her keen intellect was the reason why Detective Inspector Arthur Gottfried often consulted her regarding some of his more complex cases. She had helped with several cases that year alone and even more since she had moved to the U.K. full time from her home in Boston, Massachusetts.

Jane and Kennedy had a lot in common, making their marriage such a joy to behold. Their friends always admired the love they had for each other. Their friends often referred to their successful marriage as # *couplegoals*.

For her part, Jane was a little jealous of the families that their friends were raising, but she never let it show. She was happy being 'fun aunty Jane' for the time being. Jane would love nothing more than to have a child before her biological clock started to slow down. Lately, this had begun to be more of a pressing issue for Jane, though on the surface, she'd accepted that this was not quite the right time for the Daniels family to have children. Almost frantically, she buried herself in sleuthing and finding new gadgets to help them in their daily life and around the home as if that were enough.

Until it wasn't.

———

"Okay, Hon," Jane said before closing the garage door behind her. "There's some leftover turkey sandwiches in the fridge for your lunch and some laundry for you to fold...." She paused as Kennedy walked over to give her a peck on the cheek.

Kennedy smiled at her wife. "Don't break the bank," she told her gently, "and stay safe, okay?"

"I'll be fine; no need to worry. When do I ever break the bank? My superpower is bargain hunting," Jane said, kissing Kennedy in return before rushing out the door. She didn't want to get to the store too late. Boxing Day bargain shoppers were like caged animals being set loose from the zoo. Jane wanted to avoid all that craziness. With her coffee in a to-go mug, she headed to the car, smiling and happy.

She had an extra spring in her step that morning. Christmas had been beautiful. Jane's parents, uncle, and cousins came for Christmas dinner at their house. She and Kennedy spent all day singing and dancing around the kitchen. Family was everything to the two of them, so a chance to eat, drink, and share the day with those they loved was their version of heaven. Jane was still on a bit of a Christmas high.

As she was backing out of the drive, she looked to the front door where Kennedy was leaning against the frame, arms folded against the cold, smiling back at her. Jane blew her a kiss, turned on the radio, and pulled out the driveway, ready to start her day's adventure.

The stores didn't open until eleven on Boxing Day to allow the staff a little extra time with families after Christmas. Jane didn't care that she had left her house an hour too early. She was a woman on a mission. Determined to get the best bargains and be first in line, she was armed with coffee and the latest mystery novel by her favourite author to pass the time in the queue outside the store. She wasn't going to let boredom, or the cold, stop her. Her plan was simple. She would find a good place to park near the door and settle in with her coffee and book for a bit before the crowds came. Once she spotted the first person approaching the door, she could simply follow, snagging a place at the front of the line. She'd used the same plan every year, and it always went off without a hitch.

———

The roads were jam-packed for Boxing Day, even for London. Even though it was still early, finding a place to park wasn't easy. Jane circled the car park several times before finding the perfect spot. Not too close to the doors where her car would get dinged by busy and impatient shoppers, but not so far that she would be reduced to dragging all her heavy bags.

I don't believe this! These people must have slept in their cars to be here so early, Jane mused. Her plan to sit and read while waiting in line was now a thing of the past. She shrugged the thought away, not letting anything dampen her mood. So what if she couldn't read? The game was afoot. Soon she'd be exploring all the enormous post-Christmas bargains. She grabbed her coffee and bag and headed to the shopping centre's main entrance.

These people don't know the bargain-hunting menace that is Jane Daniels, she thought to herself, smiling as she trotted across the car park.

She made it to the big glass double doors just as they opened. A herd of people swarmed in behind her as if their very lives depended on it. Black Friday and Boxing Day sales always made people a bit crazy. She smiled to herself as she noticed the look of dread on the faces of the poor security guards. It would be a long day for the already-harried men.

The speaker system still played Christmas songs, and she hummed on her way to the men's department, where she planned to begin.

Knowing how determined Jane could be when on a mission for a bargain, her family and friends often gave her a list of items to look for. This shopping trip was no exception. She pulled up the list on her phone, quickly reading it over for the hundredth time and making a mental list she could check off as she went. With a very specific thought in mind, she made a beeline for the men's accessories first.

The men's department wasn't too busy, so she walked around with gentle ease, not having to worry about people impatiently bumping into her or fighting her to get to items. Her mind flashed to the previous Boxing Day when she'd watched two young women in their twenties get into a fight over the last discounted designer handbag.

"I saw it first!" one girl had screamed.

"No, I touched it first. It's mine!" replied the other.

Jane laughed to herself, remembering the security guards struggling to separate the women and the curses that were flung by the pair as other shoppers tutted their disapproval.

Jane often thought bargain shopping was a spectator sport. There was always drama when two women locked eyes on the same item. It was like a duel in those old western movies her father loved. The equivalent of who could unholster their gun first was the person who could grab the item first. When bargain hunting, people-watching was half the fun.

She wasn't in the men's department long before finding a lovely cashmere scarf she knew her father-in-law would love. At seventy per cent off, it was a steal, so she bought one that was gaily striped in three different colours. Then, she spotted a pair of silver and black onyx cuff-links that made her think of her uncle Leonard.

These will be perfect. He loves those retro shirts, she thought to herself, closing the box and popping them into her shopping cart along with the scarf. With the men's department checked off her list, she worked her way to the women's jewellery department, which was a lot busier, as Jane expected.

Lucia, Jane's cousin, mentioned over Christmas dinner that she wanted a silver charm bracelet. "I saw Miley at work had the cutest charm bracelet. I've wanted one ever since," she had said as she took another bite of turkey.

"Hi, how may I help you?" asked the sales clerk.

"I'm looking for a silver charm bracelet," Jane said with a smile.

"Lovely, follow me," the sales clerk said, moving around the counter and pulling out a black velvet tray with a selection of bracelets. Jane focused on the display tray in front of her.

So many choices, she thought. *Which one would Lucia like best?* Jane picked up a delicate bracelet with a selection of charms, each repre-senting different landmarks. The Eiffel Tower, the Statue of Liberty, and many more hung from the delicate chain.

"I'll take that one, please," she said, and the sales clerk headed to the back to collect a gift box. Jane moved across the counter, examining what else was on display, when someone knocked into her pushing her forward. Jane fell with such force that she banged her hip on the counter, but when she turned around to confront the pusher, they had disappeared into the crowd. "Rude much?" Jane asked aloud, shaking her head.

Jane was still rubbing her hip when the sales clerk handed her the wrapped package. She smiled and thanked her. Jane was not about to allow a momentary distraction to keep her from her mission.

Her next stop was the handbag counter. Leslie always complained that she could never find a bag with a strap long enough to pass over her head. "They're either too big or too fancy for just a morning out shopping," her mom had iterated many times. Jane had bought her mother several bags with strap lengths of varying sizes over the years, but none seemed to be what her mother had in mind.

"You have this idea in your head of what you want, but you're so set on it, nothing else will compare," Jane said once, tired of hearing the same speech about straps repeatedly.

I'm going to find one you can't complain about this year, Jane thought. As she entered the department, she spotted a bag that she thought would fit the bill. But little did she know that *a thought* was all it would be.

Just as she was about to reach the counter, one of the security guards she remembered seeing at the front entrance was blocking her path. His face was severe and determined. Confused, she halted and offered up a questioning smile. "Yes?"

He didn't smile back.

Her gut told her something was wrong, but she knew she had done nothing wrong. Had she hit him with her trolly? "So sorry. I should be more careful about where I'm going." Jane said, trying to move around the large man, but he stopped her by grabbing her trolly firmly and demanding her attention.

"I'm sorry, Miss, but can I see your bag?" he asked a little too loudly for Jane's comfort. Shoppers nearby had stopped to watch. Jane could feel their eyes burning into her. She frowned back at him, frustration and embarrassment ruining her good mood for the day.

"You mean my shopping bags or my handbag?" she asked, confused and uncertain about where this was going.

"Would you like to follow me to the office? We'll be more comfortable there," the guard said by way of a reply. He took Jane by the arm and guided her to the security office.

He was a bit taller than Jane. Even in her heeled boots, she felt she needed extra height or at least longer legs to keep up with him. His grip was firm and uncomfortable. Jane was starting to feel more and more like a common criminal and was mortified to be escorted like a naughty child, especially given that she knew for a fact she hadn't done anything wrong.

It seemed to take forever to get there. The security office was at the back of the store, close to the café on the first floor. She had been apprehended on the second floor, which meant that she was about to be paraded the length of not just one floor, but two. She wasn't looking forward to having a fresh set of eyes judging her on every floor. She frequented that particular shopping centre a lot. She worried about how she could show her face inside again.

CHAPTER 2
BEHIND LOCKED DOORS

JANE DIDN'T APPRECIATE THE SHOPPERS' accusations and judgemental looks as the security guard shoved her through the centre of the store before they reached the security office. He sat her in a small empty room with nothing inside except a table and four chairs. The room was cold and overly bright compared to the rest of the store.

"Wait here. I'll be back in a minute," he said, slamming the door behind him.

Jane heard the click of the lock before his footsteps became inaudible.

Why ask me to wait here if you are going to lock me in? Jane thought to herself. She knew her conscience was clear, so she didn't bother worrying herself silly. *This mess will be sorted out in no time. Of course, I intend to speak to the manager about how I've been treated.* She shifted about, making herself as comfortable as she could in the small plastic chairs.

A few minutes passed before the security guard joined her again with another colleague. Without saying a word, they both sat opposite her. Their expressions gave nothing away. Their faces were unreadable. Then, without saying a word, they emptied her shopping bags one by one onto the table. Next came her handbag.

"Do you have any other receipts?" the second guard asked as he shifted through the ones he'd collected from the bags. Jane glanced at his I.D. badge before answering. *Bobbi Saunders*. She made a mental note of his name.

They all looked down at the shining ruby, diamond and sapphire bracelet that fell from Jane's handbag, clattering on the table with the few other items she had inside. The two guards shared a glance before turning back to Jane.

"I have a receipt for everything, except for that bracelet, Sir," Jane answered, a little more annoyed than she intended to be that day. "I have never set eyes on that bracelet before it fell out of my bag just now."

As soon as the words left her lips, Jane realised how guilty that statement sounded.

The guard she was most angry at for his display earlier, whose name tag read *Ben Miles*, looked over to his colleague. His expression was blank.

"Why don't you go back on the floor while I wait for the police to take Mrs Daniels in for questioning?" Ben said. Without hesitation, Bobbi nodded and left, still without uttering a single word, leaving Ben and Jane alone.

Ben took on the good cop approach, sitting opposite Jane and smiling sweetly. It was so cliché that it might have been funny had the situation not been so serious.

"It's just me, now. If you can tell me what happened, we won't need to get the police involved. You seem like a respectable woman. I know you must have a good reason for doing this."

Jane folded her arms, "I'm telling the truth, and when the police get here, they will see that too," she said calmly, even as her heart began to race at the thought of being officially arrested.

———

Jane wished the security guards hadn't taken her phone before the police arrived to take her to the police station. She needed to contact Detective Inspector Arthur Gottfried to ask him what she should do under these circumstances. No. She revised this thought almost immediately. Not D.I. Arthur Gottfried. What Jane really wanted was to call Kennedy.

She would know what I should do.

The whole situation was beyond frustrating. Jane had always thought she would know how to react if she was ever arrested for a crime she hadn't committed. She'd watched enough crime shows and solved enough mysteries to know how things worked. She'd seen herself as brave, ready to stand her ground and fight her case. In no time at all, the situation would come clear, and the police would see that she was innocent. But now that she was actually in one of her imaginary scenarios, reality set in. In truth, she was terrified and floundering badly. Everything she wanted to say sounded trite now, or worse, like something that would only get her into deeper trouble.

So, she clamped her lips shut and refused to say another word while they transported her from the store.

The police station was bustling with activity, teeming with youths arrested for throwing snowballs at police cars and drunks still affected by their antics from the night before. And here was Jane, arrested for shoplifting.

The police officer led Jane through the station to the processing desk, where a female officer took her details and assigned Jane a cell before she was escorted to the interview room. The police were wasting no time trying to get to the bottom of the situation.

Jane had watched her fair share of crime documentaries and knew a bit about the criminal justice system from her time with Kennedy. She was sure she had never heard of a shoplifter being processed and interviewed so quickly. The whole situation felt strange and unnatural. Even if the bracelet had been immensely expensive, it didn't seem entirely on par with what had to be more pressing or important crimes.

An officer named Carlos Montoya escorted her into the grey, cold interview room when a thought occurred to her.

"Can I make a phone call? It's my right. I get a phone call," she said, trying to hide the fear in her voice.

Officer Montoya bent over the table, getting closer than Jane was comfortable with, and said, "You'll get your phone call soon enough, Mrs Daniels. First, I'd like to know why you stole this bracelet."

He dangled the ruby bracelet in front of her face, but the jewellery was so close to Jane's eyes that she couldn't focus on it properly.

"It's an estate bracelet worth more than a quarter of a million pounds..." he continued. He watched Jane closely, examining every facial expression, every move she made. He was waiting and looking for a clue to use against her, searching for signs of guilt; she knew what he was doing. Finally, he chuckled and sat back in his chair, staring Jane down, and said, "But you knew that, didn't you, Mrs Daniels?"

This can't be happening. Jane struggled to keep her face still, to show no sign that could be interpreted as guilt while her mind reeled. *A quarter of a million pounds?*

Officer Montoya was still waiting for a response. Jane shook her head, too stunned to come up with an answer.

CHAPTER 3
THE MORRIS BRACELET MYSTERY

ARTHUR'S MORNING had been a busy one. This time of year usually was. December typically had more crime than any other month of the year. This December was no exception, especially when it came to robberies.

He used to love the Holiday season. But as his job became more stressful, he stopped looking forward to it and started wishing it would be over sooner rather than later. He was strolling through the police station heading to his office with a pile of paperwork from his latest case when he walked past the interview room. The red light above the door was lit, indicating an interview in progress. He had walked past three interview rooms on his journey through the station. As he passed interview room four, his instincts told him to take a peek.

He glanced in the small box window and noticed a face he recognised in the chair where suspects usually sat. He froze in his tracks, taking a second look. The woman was a brunette, a little shorter than the average woman, and had *terrified* blue eyes. His eyes were not playing tricks on him; it was Mrs Daniels. Not wasting another second, he stormed through the door, startling the Officer and Mrs Daniels.

"Officer Montoya," he said as evenly as his flaring temper would allow. "May I have a word?"

Officer Montoya nodded, giving Mrs Daniels a stern look before exiting the room with D.I. Arthur.

"Why are you interviewing Mrs Daniels?" Arthur asks, his brow furrowed. He struggled to keep a professional tone, but his anger got the better of him, and he spoke sharper than he intended.

Officer Montoya lowered his gaze. Everyone in the police station knew D.I. Gottfried was not someone whose temper you got on the wrong side of. And Montoya had a reputation of being cocky and often too hard when interviewing suspects.

"She's been caught red-handed, Detective. She had Mrs Evelyn Morris' bracelet in her bag...." Montoya replied.

Arthur was speechless for the first time in as long as he could remember. He replayed the officer's words in his head one more time, analysing them. He wasn't sure he had heard his colleague correctly and needed to be sure before asking his next question.

"Are you saying that Mrs Daniels swiped a bracelet from the estate display at the store?" Arthur asked, eyes wide, still in a state of disbelief.

Officer Montoya nodded emphatically. Arthur took a second to think of what to ask next. He didn't want to believe Mrs Daniels could do such a thing.

"Did the security guard see her take it?" Arthur asked finally.

"No, Sir, security didn't see her take it. They were alerted when one of the sales clerks pressed the alarm under the counter," Montoya answered, his stance relaxing somewhat as though he were confident of his answer.

"Has anyone checked the CCTV footage? Is there any evidence of her taking it?" Arthur asked, frowning.

"Yes, we reviewed the footage. No, Sir, she wasn't seen taking it. She was pushed into the display, though. It could have been premeditated. A distraction to throw the trail off of her."

Arthur nodded, taking another moment to think things over. This was a very sensitive issue, even without one of his close friends getting caught in the middle of it. Arthur wracked his brain, trying to think of a scenario that made sense to him as to why Mrs Jane Daniels would be involved or how a woman like her could have gotten mixed up in this kind of a mess.

"Let me speak with Mrs Daniels before you do anything else, okay?" Arthur said calmly. Officer Montoya opened the door. Arthur handed him his pile of paperwork, and he entered the room alone.

Mrs Daniels slumped in her chair, defeated as she sat staring at her hands clasped in front of her on the table. She hadn't even noticed him walk in. He stood just past the doorway for a moment or two, watching her. When she finally looked up, her expression and posture relaxed as she sat back in her chair, taking an audible sigh of relief.

"I never thought I'd see a friendly face around here," Jane said, frustration dripping off every word as Arthur pulled out the chair opposite her.

Arthur sat, leaning his forearms on the table. "Well, let's say I'm only a little concerned at this point." He paused for a second to watch her reaction. He tried to stay impartial, but his detective instincts wouldn't allow him to. Something felt off about this whole thing.

"Just tell me what happened right before you were apprehended," he said gently. Jane sighed again, glancing down at her lap again before returning her gaze to meet Arthur's, her eyes pleading with him.

"Well, I was shopping for Lucia's gift, and I was standing against the counter waiting for the sales clerk to wrap my purchase when someone pushed me against the counter. It's Boxing Day madness, so I just assumed it was a rude shopper. I didn't think about it again until the security guard paraded me through the store like a common criminal. The rest, you know."

It wasn't much to work with. Arthur didn't like seeing his friend in such a distressed state. Mrs Daniels was a sweet woman who had given up her job in graphic design when she got married, hoping to start a family. She was kind-hearted and generous and often went out of her way to help people. She was the polar opposite of the type of person who would commit a crime. But Arthur needed to think clearly and get to the bottom of this mystery if he was going to help her. To do that, he would need to keep his emotions in check. That meant staying impartial until he knew she was in the clear. Unfortunately, the best way for him to do that was, at least for the time being, to treat Jane as if she was guilty.

CHAPTER 4
A DANGEROUS DISTRACTION

"I SEE. Could you describe the person who pushed you?" Arthur asked.

Jane shook her head, staring down at her lap again.

How was she supposed to clear her name if she couldn't give them any information? If she couldn't clear her name, what would happen to her? Would she go to jail? Her mind raced as fast as her pulse.

She knew enough about the law and how the police interrogated suspects. Even the innocent could look guilty if they panicked or showed the slightest weakness. Anything the police could use to close the case, they would. Their aim was always to make a person crack, to spill all their secrets enough so the truth would finally come to light.

She was on the verge of a panic attack and needed to calm down.

"No, not really," she started. "I remember feeling a hand at my back. I was pushed into the counter, and I bashed my hip. When I turned around, an older fellow in a brown coat was hurrying away from the jewellery department before I lost him in the crowd," she said, closing her eyes as she tried to remember the scene more clearly.

She had seen once in a documentary that it was a technique called cognitive interview, which had been proven to reliably enhance the process of memory retrieval. She was glad to discover that it worked.

After that, however, curiosity started to rear its head, and Jane wondered what the man in the brown coat had to do with the bracelet and, more importantly, why he'd gotten her involved in this mess.

"Okay, Jane. I'm going to have you released with a caution only. You will need to stay home for the rest of the day. I'll come by later tonight to tell you the story of the Morris Bracelet," Arthur said, and Jane nodded, dangerously near crying as she finally allowed herself to relax.

Her shoulders ached from how tense she had become, and despite her best efforts, tears were starting to well up in her eyes, blurring her vision. It was so overwhelming. Before she became any more overwhelmed, she took a careful breath, nodded, and left without asking anything further. She just wanted to go home and press herself against Kennedy. She always felt safe in Kennedy's arms.

———

Jane hadn't been home for ten minutes before the doorbell rang. Kennedy jumped up to answer it. Glancing over her shoulder at her wife, whose face was pale and pinched with anxiety, she said, "You stay right there, hon. You never know with the police...." She didn't want to worry Jane any further, but she felt like she had to prepare her all the same.

When Jane arrived home after the incident at the shopping centre, she was a mess of tears and heaving sobs. Jane was usually the person who could light up any room she walked into. Seeing her like that broke Kennedy's heart.

In their wedding vows, she had promised to protect Jane from anything that could harm her or dim her light. Now Kennedy worried about how she would keep her wife from going to prison for a theft she didn't commit.

Get a grip, Kennedy. Focus on the facts. You need to be strong for Jane, she thought before she opened the door.

Her friend Detective Inspector Arthur Gottfried stood outside. "Good evening, Arthur," Kennedy chirped, trying her best not to show her concerns, though his serious expression gave her pause. Whatever he had to say, she sensed it wouldn't be good.

"Hi," Arthur replied, stepping inside. "Jane told you I would be coming round this evening, right?" he asked, removing his coat and hanging it up on the coat rack behind the door the way he had on a hundred other visits.

Kennedy nodded vigorously, her black ringlets bouncing with every nod. "That she did. She's in the living room."

Arthur nodded and walked down the hallway to the archway leading to the living room. "Arthur!" Jane exclaimed, getting up from the sofa. "Coffee and cake are all ready for you. Please sit down," she said, indicating a cosy chair across from her. "I hope you don't mind a Victoria sponge. I baked it earlier."

Kennedy smiled. It was such a Jane thing to do, to play the welcoming hostess despite her fears. Of course, nothing kept Jane down for long. It was one of the things that Kennedy loved most about her.

After Kennedy had managed to calm Jane down when she arrived home, Jane did what she always did when stressed. She shut the world out, cleaned the house from top to bottom, and then spent the rest of her time baking in the kitchen. By the time Arthur arrived, Jane had baked a Victoria sponge, a batch of chocolate chip cookies, and a loaf of raisin bread.

It was something her mother had taught her to do. "Find some-thing else for your mind to focus on" had been almost a mantra at Jane's house growing up. The intense activity usually worked. When she was done, her mind would be ready for intense concentration, and she could work through whatever issue had been stressing her.

But this time, it seemed nothing could calm the chaos in Jane's mind. No task she completed appeared to be enough. It unsettled Kennedy, and she didn't know what she could do to help her wife other than to stand back and watch while Jane ran herself ragged.

Kennedy sat down next to her wife, helped her pour three cups of coffee, and served the cake. Once everyone was settled, she took her wife's hand in hers. Then, squeezing tightly, she gave her a silent signal saying, *I'm here for you. I've got you. You're safe, and I love you.*

Jane looked over, smiling weakly; she squeezed Kennedy's hand in return. *I love you too.*

They both sat waiting for Arthur's news.

For better or worse, Kennedy replayed in her mind, squeezing Jane's hand a little tighter. They all sat quietly for a few minutes, ignoring the elephant in the room. They each were awkwardly digging into the cake, waiting for someone to break the silence.

Arthur took a bite of his cake and a sip of his coffee before he began, "I'm sorry for what happened to you this morning, Jane, but this is a delicate case. We were trying to attract the alleged murderer to come back for the loot…" he said.

Kennedy looked back at him blankly. This was not what she expected to hear. Her worry levels escalated immediately—her worries before paled in comparison to how she was now feeling. To be accused of theft was one thing. To be involved in a murder was next-level crazy. What would happen if Jane went to prison? *She wouldn't cope in prison,* Kennedy thought to herself.

She took a deep breath. Though her heart was breaking, she had to stay strong for Jane. She couldn't afford to think about losing Jane or the future they had planned. Their life together flashed before Kennedy's eyes. *We haven't even started our family yet. Jane was born to be a mother. This isn't fair,* she thought, fighting back the tears.

Jane interrupted, putting her coffee cup down with a clatter, mainly because her hands had begun to shake. "You mean, you're using the bracelet as some sort of bait?" she asked.

Arthur nodded. "Yes. We found the bracelet under the chest of drawers where Mrs Morris was killed. We figured the man would try to come back for it — but he didn't. So, the lieutenant suggested putting the bracelet amongst the estate jewellery in the department store and advertising it as "an item of great value belonging to the late Mrs Morris," Arthur said, taking another sip of his coffee and eyeing another slice of cake.

Kennedy listened intently to Arthur as he went into more detail about what the police had been trying to do by setting the trap. It was an exciting plan, but there were so many ways for it to go wrong.

"I don't see why the murderer would risk getting caught stealing a bracelet that he must know is under guard day and night," she said. "If you have no real leads and nothing much else to go on, he or she has essentially gotten away with murder. Why would they risk being caught even if the bracelet is worth a small fortune?" Kennedy asked.

Kennedy noticed out of the corner of her eye that Jane was sitting on the edge of her seat, watching them both closely, as though waiting for the piece of information that would mean she was off the hook.

Arthur swallowed a bite of his second slice of cake before continuing. "I understand your thinking, but we thought that anyone interested in the bracelet might want to handle it or ask the clerk to show it to them. The security cameras are all focusing on the estate jewellery counter...."

Jane held up her hand, interrupting Arthur. "Then why was I arrested in public if the guards knew I didn't steal it? The CCTV should clearly show that I'm innocent," Jane said, her annoyance plain for all to see.

Kennedy couldn't blame her wife for being upset. She had a valid point. The stress Jane had been put through was unnecessary. The more Kennedy thought about what her wife had been through, the more annoyed she became.

Kennedy turned sharply towards Arthur. Her brow furrowed. "Hold up a minute. If the bracelet was under CCTV surveillance twenty-four-seven, how did anyone remove the bracelet in the first place? How could you miss that?" she snapped.

She didn't mean to snap at Arthur. He had been her friend for over fifteen years.

Arthur held his hands up in surrender. "Calm down, Kennedy. I knew that point wouldn't slip past you. The CCTV on the second floor wasn't turned on when we realised the bracelet was missing. The sales clerk pointed at Jane simply because she was there when she realised the bracelet was missing. She was the only one near the counter that was taking any real interest in jewellery at the time. Again, I'm sorry Jane was caught up in all of this," Arthur said.

CHAPTER 5
SECRETS IN THE CCTV

.

JANE STARED AT ARTHUR. As far as apologies go, it wasn't exactly satisfying.

"Caught up in?" Kennedy was not exactly mollified either, judging by her tone.

"Because we needed to let the real thief think that we had apprehended our thief," Arthur said.

Jane shook her head. "But that doesn't make sense, Arthur. Why not take the bracelet and make a run for it?"

Until now, Jane had felt like she was watching a tennis match as her head whipped back and forth between Kennedy and Arthur. She had questions and was getting tired of not speaking up for herself.

"Jane is right. If he already had the bracelet, and no one had grabbed him for it, why not make a run for it, or even stash it somewhere and come back another day?" Kennedy asked.

Arthur grimaced, "The thief knows that security would likely chase after him, and he would be caught red-handed. The man in the brown coat couldn't risk that. Being caught thieving is one thing. Being arrested in connection with a murder investigation is another."

Kennedy and Jane shared a look. Arthur had a point. His plan may have seemed a little far-fetched, but in the long run, it all made sense.

And when you didn't have much else to go on, the only way to catch a fish was to dangle a worm on a hook.

Jane relaxed on the sofa, trying to make sense of everything Arthur had said. She was now in the clear. At least she didn't have to worry about going to jail for a crime she hadn't committed. She suppressed a yawn. She knew she would sleep well that night.

Well, maybe not. Now that her brain was worry-free, her inner Detective kicked in; the cogs in her brain started to turn. "I still don't understand," she said. "Arthur, what would the man gain from dropping the bracelet into my shopping bag if he knew I would be caught? He still wouldn't have access to the bracelet and...."

Suddenly, the light bulb in Jane's mind came on as an idea popped into her head.

"He knew he wouldn't have to worry about you looking for him in the store. I was his scapegoat," she said, sighing and running her hands over her face.

"Except that we've replaced the bracelet in the display case this afternoon," Arthur continued.

Jane was becoming more and more confused. She prided herself on solving a good mystery, but this didn't even begin to make sense. Anyone who knew anything about how the police worked would expect the bracelet to be locked up in evidence right now.

"You are trying to bait him again?" Kennedy asked.

Jane knew where Kennedy was going with this. She couldn't understand how Arthur could think that if a plan hadn't worked once, it might work this time.

"Actually, we want someone to buy the damn thing. One of our undercover officers will do that tomorrow. We hope that the suspect will attack the officer, trying to steal the bracelet back. When that happens, we will finally have him in custody," Arthur said.

Jane looked over to Kennedy, the pair sharing a glance. They had to admit it was a good plan. Jane wanted a little more clarification, "So, you believe the man in the brown coat is going to follow the officer to his car and attempt to rob him before he leaves the car park, is that right?"

That's when another thought occurred to Jane. Maybe being apprehended by the security guard and taken to the police station was a blessing in disguise. If she had left the shopping centre with the bracelet in her bag, the murderer would probably have attacked *her*. The thought sent a cold shiver down her spine. One of her worst fears was being robbed on the streets of London. But, of course, this was why ignorance is bliss. She would rather not know how close she had been to her worst fear becoming a reality.

Arthur nodded, looking rather pleased with his plan. "Pretty much, yes. Once we have him, we can question the man regarding the murder," he said.

Jane shook her head. She couldn't believe what she was hearing. How quickly Arthur was willing to put someone else in danger. The man in the brown coat was clearly dangerous. What if he had killed Mrs Morris? How did they expect to keep their undercover cop safe in all of this?

"Mrs Morris fought the suspect. We found skin cells under her fingernails, indicating she likely scratched his face or neck. If we could get a look at the man in the brown coat, we could confirm if he is the murderer or not," Arthur said matter-of-factly.

The three friends fell silent, stopping for a second to take in the information shared that evening.

"Was the bracelet the only thing the suspect was supposed to have stolen?" Kennedy asked. Arthur shook his head with a slight grin on his face. He knew Kennedy well enough to know where her mind was at. Her mystery-solving curiosity had been piqued. She was already dissecting everything, trying to piece it all back together again. Arthur knew Kennedy was like a dog with a bone when it came to a case like this. She wouldn't stop until it was solved.

Since working with Kennedy, the number of unsolved cases in the area had been drastically reduced.

"No, he surprised Mrs Morris when she opened the safe in her bedroom. She had been to a reception that evening at the mayor's house. She was putting her jewels away when he attacked," he explained. Arthur pulled a small notebook from his pocket and flipped over a few pages before he continued. "There was a pair of earrings and a ruby necklace, with sapphires and diamonds too, to match the bracelet and a few pieces with a lower value."

Jane's face lit up with curiosity. Scooting forward, she asked, "Do you have pictures of the stolen items?"

Arthur nodded. Pulling his phone out of his pocket, he loaded up the pictures and passed his phone over to Jane.

"Here they are," he said. Jane studied the images swiping from one to the other. Despite the jewellery being worth a small fortune, she knew there had to be more to this murder than a simple robbery. These gems had a history, a story to tell. Now that she was off the hook, she intended to sink her teeth into the mystery that was Mrs Morris' jewels.

CHAPTER 6
THE MILAN CONNECTION

THE FOLLOWING DAY, it was business as usual at the store. The staff set out to make the store look presentable for the next rush of customers. The staff in the jewellery department had just finished polishing the display cabinets when the security guards opened the doors to welcome the first customers of the day. The scene was set.

In a polished mahogany box in the centre of the cabinet in the jewellery department, there was a white gold bracelet set with rubies, diamonds, and sapphires—a truly beautiful piece.

The sales clerk smiled, greeting the tall, handsome stranger that approached her counter. He had striking blue eyes and dark wavy hair with a debonair allure about him. When he smiled at her, she gave him a shy smile as she tucked a strand of hair behind her ear. The handsome stranger looked over the items in her display case before raising his eyes to meet hers.

"Would you mind showing me the bracelet with rubies and sapphires?" he asked, pointing to Mrs Morris' bracelet.

"Not at all, Sir," the clerk replied, inserting the key for the display case into the lock.

She pulled on a pair of white cotton gloves as it was store policy for any high-value jewellery to be handled as such. She removed the bracelet delicately from the cabinet and placed it on a black velvet tray. The dark velvet highlighted the bracelet's beauty and the sparkle of the diamonds. The white gold setting seemed to sparkle more against the dark background. She gently pushed the tray closer to the customer. He leaned over, inspecting it closely. He pulled out a jeweller's eyeglass to inspect each stone closely, checking the diamonds for inclusions to ascertain each stone's quality. He made small talk in between, asking questions about the Four C's: colour, cut, clarity, and colour. The sales clerk answered each question with ease, and each response was met with a satisfied nod.

"What is the asking price for this item," he asked, standing back to his full height, just a little taller than the sales clerk, forcing her to angle her neck slightly to look at him.

"Two hundred and fifty thousand pounds, Sir," she replied with a smile.

"That's fine. Please wrap it up...I hope your manager will not mind taking a cheque?" he asked with a smile.

"That's fine, Sir. With purchases of this size, we favour cheques over cash," the sales clerk said with a smile as she boxed up the bracelet.

The sales clerk would generally be ecstatic with an item of this value. The commission of that item alone would be more than two months' pay. But today was not her day. She and the rest of her team had been made aware that the handsome gentleman in front of her was a police officer trying to catch a suspect. Nonetheless, she went through the motions of checking his identification before handing him the signature white bag with a red velvet bow. If it felt strange to her to conduct this transaction so casually, ignoring several store protocols for such a large purchase, she gave no sign.

The officer took his new purchase and headed towards the lifts, pressing the button for the car park. Subtly, he looked around, scanning his surroundings, watching every customer in the store, looking for his mark. Finally, the doors opened, and he stepped inside, a little disappointed that their sting hadn't gone quite as planned.

Just as the doors were about to close, a tall man in a brown coat rushed in beside him. *This is the guy. He matches the CCTV footage,* the officer thought, keeping his eyes fixed on the double doors.

"Hey buddy, you've just bought something that belongs to me," the suspect said calmly to the officer. The officer smirked and cocked an eyebrow, turning towards the suspect almost as if making idle conversation. Like, what the guy had said didn't matter. "Oh really? And what would that be?" he asked.

The suspect reached into his coat pocket and retrieved a long, steel kitchen knife.

"The bracelet," he said with a sneer.

The lift jolted to a stop, and the double doors opened with a ping. They'd arrived at the car park level. The suspect hadn't been paying attention and was startled as the door opened, revealing an entire army of cops. Clearly, he hadn't been expecting them to make it to the car park so quickly, nor that they would have company when they did. The officer used this to his advantage.

While the suspect glanced at the commotion outside the doors, the officer pushed him hard into the wall knocking the knife out of his hands before tossing him to the floor. The suspect tried to fight back, kicking and flailing his arms while trying to land a punch, but the officer was too quick. Two hard and fast punches to the face immobilised the suspect. It was over.

"Finally!" the officer exclaimed, shaking off his punching hand. He stepped aside while the rest of the police officers in the car park rushed to his aid. Two young officers picked the suspect up, cuffed his hands, and read him his rights before taking him into custody. Within moments, he had been placed in the back of the police car and was on his way to the station.

———

Arthur sat back in his chair in the interview room, not believing a word coming out of the man's mouth. The suspect's name was Sam Torkin, and the tales he was weaving left Arthur in disbelief.

"That Morris woman was the thief," Sam insisted, getting increasingly animated the more he retold his version of events.

"She took the jewels out of my mother's case when I was just a boy. When I tried to get them back, she just laughed at me, saying I imagined it," Sam said, running his hands through his hair.

He had to know his story would sound far-fetched. Arthur didn't believe it for a second.

"See, Detective, we had a nice house and all good things in life, but my dad was a bit of a gambler. He lost the family fortune in a poker game. One day we're living the high life; the next, we're on the street. But before that happened, my mother had a maid by the name of Louisa Morris. She took the jewellery from my mum. I was only taking back what was mine," Sam insisted.

"You expect us to believe that?" Arthur said with a grin. He shouldn't have found the story so entertaining. He was investigating a woman's murder, after all. But he couldn't help thinking that this was one of the best excuses he'd heard in a long time.

"I never meant to hurt her. It was an accident. I just wanted my family's jewels back," Sam said.

"Tell me again what happened," Arthur said. He had asked Sam three times, and three times Sam had answered. Arthur had a reason for his repetition. He was looking for variations in Sam's story, hoping to spot anything he could use to find out the truth.

Sam sighed, trying his hardest to control his temper. "I've told you how many times now? Do I have to tell you again?" he asked.

Arthur crossed his arms and nodded.

"I spent years tracking her down. When I knocked on her door, she didn't recognise me at first. Once I'd explained who I was, she invited me to wait in the living room. I couldn't believe she was wearing the jewels. She said she'd be back in a moment.

I waited for a beat and followed her to her room… She was startled and started screaming for me to leave," he said.

Arthur nodded, indicating he should continue.

"She started hitting me, screaming for me to get out. I said I was taking back what was mine. She tried to stop me. She was unsteady on her feet. She slipped and banged her head on the dressing table," Sam said, trailing off, pausing to rub his eyes. It was getting harder and harder for him to relive the events.

"Continue," Arthur said, urging him on. Sam sighed and ran his hand over his face.

"She was bleeding. There was so much blood I didn't know what to do. I grabbed what I could and just ran. I knew how it looked. I was too scared to call the police or phone an ambulance. How was I going to explain why I was there?" he said.

Arthur was sure he heard a sob. A twang of guilt and remorse in his voice. Was this guy for real?

Arthur didn't want to admit it, but he believed Sam. And he wasn't won over easily. He knew there were those who could cry on demand, and thieves and murderers could be fairly credible actors. He needed to dig to see if Sam's story had any merit. What if the man was telling the truth? Not that it would change the outcome by much. A woman was dead either way. But there was a difference between manslaughter and murder. It was his duty to check it out.

He already knew the perfect person for the job. If anyone could get to the bottom of all this, it would be Kennedy Daniels.

CHAPTER 7
THE HEIST UNRAVELED

ARTHUR HAD TASKED Kennedy with checking out Sam Torkin's story by doing a background check on Mrs Morris. Kennedy always worked better on her own, so she decided to do her research at home. The idea of working with the rest of the cyber research team in that stuffy, crowded room in the police station made her skin crawl. The noise. The mindless chatter. How was she expected to concentrate with people over her shoulder and shoving their opinions in her face?

She spent hours digging deep into Mrs Morris' life. She found out about her three failed marriages, messy divorces, and all the places around the world she had lived during her life.

Kennedy investigated her medical history and checked if she had a criminal record. She searched for any information she could find on the jewels. They turned out to be a pretty unique set, so there was bound to be some information about them.

If what Sam said was true, there would be a record of his family owning them at one point: receipts, a paper trail. Kennedy loved a good paper trail. It made her job that much easier. Then, she dug a little deeper into Mrs Morris' education, financial records, and finally, her employment history.

When Kennedy finished researching the Morris family's past, she turned to Jane. Jane was engrossed in a book about famous European jewellery pieces. Kennedy thought her wife looked so beautiful when concentrating like she was. Her nose would wrinkle, and without realising, she would purse her lips while reading. Kennedy watched her for a second longer before she said, "Sorry to draw you out of your book, hon, but I think I've worked out the mystery surrounding the bracelet and necklace."

Jane snapped the book shut and turned her eager face toward Kennedy. "What did you find out?"

"Originally, they belonged to the Twentieth-Century Italian Jewellery Exhibit at the Poldi Pezzoli Museum in Milan. Unfortunately, the thieves who stole the bracelet and necklace were never caught, and the jewellery was never recovered. So perhaps we're looking at a piece of history that should be returned to Italy?" she said.

Jane's eyes widened before her face lit up with excitement.

"Are you serious? Wow, who would have thought this went so deep? Never in a million years would I have thought I'd be caught in the middle of something so exciting. Well, apart from the death of Mrs Morris, of course," she said, putting her book aside and sliding across the sofa to peer over Kennedy's shoulder to look at her laptop screen.

"I wouldn't say you were caught in the middle. Thankfully, you are more like a concerned passer-by. But I see your point. I better call Arthur. He needs to hear about this pronto," Kennedy said quickly, kissing Jane on the cheek before passing the laptop over to her. She knew Jane would be fascinated with the history of the jewels and would want to read the articles she'd found for herself.

Kennedy grabbed her mobile from the coffee table and dialled D.I. Gottfried's number. He answered after two rings, "Hi Arthur, you are not going to believe what I found out...sure, come on over, I'll put the kettle on," she said before ending the call.

CHAPTER 8
A NEW YEAR IN MILAN

ARTHUR CAME over that night to look over Kennedy's findings. Jane did all she could to keep from interjecting. This was Kennedy's triumph, not hers. She pressed her lips firmly together and calmly served the cake.

"What did you find, Kennedy?" Arthur asked as Jane poured him a cup of tea.

"Mr Torkin was telling the truth. Mrs Morris did work for his family," Kennedy said.

"How did his family gain possession of the jewels? Do you think they were involved in the original theft?" he asked.

Kennedy shrugged. "No idea. The case on that one is still cold, and there weren't many leads for me to go on," Kennedy replied. "So far, I haven't been able to connect the theft with their possession of the jewels. Whether they bought them legitimately, got them from a fence somehow, or even stole them themselves, it's impossible to say just yet."

"At least that part of his story checks out. I have a contact in Italy. I'll see if he knows anything. Thank you for your help, Kennedy," Arthur said.

Jane cleared her throat with a cheeky smile.

"And you too, Jane," Arthur smiled back, finishing his tea. Arthur thanked the ladies for their help and told them he would be in touch once he had more news.

Two days later, the police were made aware of the historical value of the necklace and bracelet. The relevant authorities were informed that Gottfried and the Daniels' would be making their way to Italy and the Milan Poldi Pezzoli Museum.

The Italian police were scheduled to meet them at the airport and escort them to the museum. The jewels would finally be back where they belonged.

————

"Ladies and gentlemen, the fasten seatbelts light has now been turned off, and it is safe to stretch your legs by wandering around the cabin. The cabin crew will be around shortly with the food and drinks trolly. Sit back and enjoy the rest of your journey," came the pilot's voice over the intercom system.

Arthur excused himself to join the long queue for the men's bathroom, and Kennedy sat sleeping next to Jane. Jane closed her book and looked out the window. It was night. All she could see were the stars in the sky.

What a crazy couple of days, she thought to herself as she rested her head back against her chair. *Less than a week ago, I was shopping for bargains, and now I've been involved in a murder and theft investigation, and I'm on my way to Italy. Who would have thunk it?* She smiled to herself, happy and content.

Arthur made it back before the cabin crew arrived with food and drinks. Kennedy woke up and ordered coffee for all of them, passing the air hostess her card to pay. The dark sky would break soon. Coffee would be just the thing to get the day started.

"You okay, hon?" Kennedy asked with a smile as she handed Jane her coffee.

Jane nodded enthusiastically, "I would never have thought — not in a million years — that we would be going to Milan to ring in the

New Year!" Jane said, beaming as she snuggled up against her wife. Kennedy smiled back at Jane and kissed the top of her head.

When they arrived in Milan, D.I. Arthur Gottfried, Jane, and Kennedy headed straight to the Poldi Pezzoli Museum. Jane was in awe. It was a beautiful place with traditional Northern Italian architecture; there were so many exhibits in fashion, art, and history. Jane couldn't wait to explore. They handed the jewellery over to the curator and were treated to a history lesson about the jewels and their Medici owners. Once the jewels were safely put away, the entire group was treated to a V.I.P. tour. It was a dream come true to spend New Year's Eve in such a beautiful place with such rich history with the woman she loved.

"Today has been amazing. I can't wait for the evening celebrations," Jane chirped as they sat in a café sipping espresso. They'd checked into the hotel and freshened up after their time at the museum. Their hotel was hosting a New Year's Eve party in the lounge later that night. The concierge informed them there would be a jazz ensemble, fireworks, and a midnight buffet. Jane couldn't wait.

"Come on, Kennedy. We must find something awesome to wear. How often are we going to be in Milan? I can't believe I get to shop in one of the world's fashion capitals," Jane said cheerfully, tugging on Kennedy's hand as she pulled her towards the row of boutiques. Arthur laughed and excused himself back to the hotel. "I'll leave you ladies to it. Jane, try not to get involved in any more heists while you're here. I want to enjoy my little holiday," he joked with a wink as he left.

It took an hour of bouncing from boutique to boutique and an endless stream of grumbling from Kennedy, but Jane finally found the perfect cocktail dress for the evening and a tailored jumpsuit for Kennedy. "You and your bargain hunting," Kennedy laughed as they took a scenic tour before heading back to their hotel.

"Come on, you love that jumpsuit. For the price, I couldn't let it sit there. When our friends back home find out I found you an original Versace at that price, they are just going to die of envy!"

Jane smiled. Kennedy was about to mention they were dying of envy because they couldn't afford to travel as much now that they had kids, but she thought better of it. If it was too sore a subject and it would kill the mood.

"At least you didn't break the bank," Kennedy said with a wink.

———

Everyone in the hotel gathered on the terrace for the midnight countdown. The lounge was decorated in white and gold silk. The staff were all dressed in tuxedoes and cocktail dresses decorated with white and gold accessories to match the décor. As the countdown began, Jane grabbed each of Arthur and Kennedy's hands. *"Tre...due...uno...Buon Anno!"*

Everyone cheered as fireworks lit up the sky. Noisemakers blared, and the orchestra launched into something which sounded suspiciously like "Auld Lang Syne" set to jazz as people kissed and embraced each other.

"Happy New Year, hon," Kennedy said, kissing her wife and wrapping her arms around her.

"Happy New Year," Jane replied, her body buzzing with excitement. She would always remember this very special day.

———

As for Sam Torkin, he confessed to the attempted robbery and involuntary manslaughter of Mrs Morris, in addition to attempted armed robbery against the undercover police officer. It was an open and shut case. The evidence the police had gathered, combined with the medical examiner's report, supported his story that the death had been accidental. Once the jewellery was recovered and on its way back to Italy, the judge settled the case quickly. Everyone was eager to clock out for New Year.

He was sentenced to two years in prison, commuted to 500 hours of community service and mandatory twice-weekly counselling. Given his family's history and the events that led him to commit his crime, he asked the judge if he could serve out his sentence helping at London's busiest homeless shelter.

Remembering all his Christmases as a boy, cold and homeless, thanks to his father's poor decisions, he wanted to start out the New Year right. He meant well. He really had never intended for anyone to get hurt. Things had spiralled out of control, and he ended up in too deep. He would regret his actions for the rest of his life. Thankfully, the judge had seen how remorseful Sam was and how much he wanted to repent.

Just before Jane flew off to Italy with Arthur and Kennedy, she made sure to check in on the judge's verdict. She felt invested in the case. Against her better judgement, she reached out to Sam, and when she found out about his plans, she wanted to help in any way she could.

While Jane rang in the New Year in Italy, Sam prepared a fantastic turkey dinner for all the shelter's residents. He had a local band play to make it as festive as possible. He wanted the residents to ring in the New Year with a heart full of love, clean and warm clothing, and a full belly.

Jane thought that was a lovely idea, and being the caring person that she was, she felt she needed to do something as well. After all, it could have been anyone looking at the jewellery counter that day. Jane was a firm believer in fate. Destiny had brought her and Sam together. To ensure the New Year celebrations at the shelter went off without a hitch, Jane wrote out a big fat cheque to cover all the expenses. Attached to the check was a note.

Dear Sam,
I hope this will help make New Year at the shelter one to remember. Happy New Year!
- The Daniels

The End

INJURED ON NEW YEAR'S

A COZY MYSTERY

CHAPTER 1
A GLITTERING FALL

JANE DANIELS HAD ALWAYS BEEN a bit of a sleuth. She loved mysteries, crime novels, and drama. One of her favourite pastimes was to curl up on the sofa with her wife, Kennedy, watching serial killer documentaries and trying to piece everything together before the celebrity narrator revealed who the killer was. The fact that Kennedy enjoyed the same thing was one thing that first attracted Jane to her wife. They both loved mysteries, and Jane had a talent for solving crimes. Jane looked at mysteries as though they were puzzles. She saw them as just missing that vital piece, and she needed to be the one to find it.

Jane also loved a good bargain. She loved hunting around shops for that particular bargain item she could brag about. She considered every shopping expedition an excuse to hunt for treasure. The X on her mental treasure map was always the location of the most discounted item in whatever particular store she was in. Jane loved the after-Christmas and January sales the most. All the must-have items, new gadgets, and things she could put aside for the following year were at the best possible discount price, making them a definite, *Yes, please*! It was a yearly tradition to check out what treasures she could find.

Meanwhile, Kennedy was the cyber-wizard of the family. She loved it when Jane came home with a new gadget. She loved nothing more than adding to her electronics collection, especially anything she could use to make everyday life easier and more enjoyable. Kennedy had practically automated every inch of their home. It was like living in the future, and they loved it.

Kennedy was a reasonably intelligent woman. She was very proud of her MIT education. Her keen intellect was why Detective Inspector Arthur Gottfried often consulted her regarding some of his more complex cases. She had helped with many instances that year alone, and even more since she had moved to the UK full time from her home in Boston, Massachusetts.

Jane and Kennedy had a lot in common, making their marriage a joy to behold. Their friends always admired the love they had for each other. Their friends often referred to their successful marriage as #couplegoals.

Jane used to envy her family and friends for having the one thing she didn't – A child of her own. She loved being 'fun aunty Jane' but craved being called 'Mummy' the most. After their near miss on Halloween, Jane and Kennedy had decided it was finally time to start a family. However, Jane's run-in with the law on Boxing Day had momentarily put a hold on their plans. But as the New Year approached, it signalled a fresh start, the start of the next part of their journey in life together. Jane could hardly wait.

———

Their unexpected trip to Italy had been fun and exactly what they needed after Jane was arrested on Boxing Day. Jane was glad that everything with Sam and the jewellery theft had been sorted and she could go back to life as usual.

It was time to pack up their things and return home to London. Unfortunately, since it was New Year's Day, travelling was sure to be a nightmare. The airports would be packed; Jane would have loved to stay a little longer, but a New Year's Day ticket was the only one available on such short notice. They couldn't stay for another two weeks – no matter how much Jane wanted to.

The mayor was hosting yet another ball; Jane and Kennedy had been humming and hawing over whether to attend. After the Halloween Horrors party, it would either go wonderfully, and they would be able to make new memories, or they would be forced to relive the painful ones from the judge's fatal shooting.

But Jane had never been one to turn down an invitation, and Kennedy followed wherever Jane went. So, they booked their ticket and waved goodbye to their spontaneous Italian getaway.

Jane rolled over in bed and snuggled up to Kennedy. She pushed a strand of her beautiful black ringlets out of her face and kissed her forehead. She was so lucky to have such a wonderful wife.

The hotel they were staying in was remarkably fancy. The architecture was beautiful and oozed history. While it was amazing, it was a far cry from their technologically advanced home. Jane looked to the tea and coffee facilities: a small kettle and a few packets of instant coffee, tea bags, and sugar with a small jug of milk tucked in the under-cabinet fridge. For such a short trip, it would do. Jane and Kennedy couldn't wait to get home to their coffee machine. It would have their favourite coffees freshly brewed waiting for them when they arrived – all thanks to a click of an app Kennedy had designed.

The mayor's New Year's Ball was rumoured to be just as lavish as the last. Celebrities, sports stars, and influential people were all invited. The paparazzi were even more excited about this ball after the fateful events of the Halloween party she hosted. They were hoping for an even better story this time.

"Kennedy," Jane sighed. "We must start packing to make it home in time for the mayor's ball."

Kennedy groaned and pulled a pillow over her head.

"Five more minutes..." a soft snoring sound could be heard, muffled by the pillow.

Jane chuckled and moved the pillow off Kennedy's head.

"Sorry, babe. We don't have time," she glanced at the clock. "It's already seven. The airport is going to be packed."

The pair rolled out of bed and rubbed the sleep from their eyes. Jane quickly headed to the kitchenette to brew fresh coffees. The strong aroma filled the room. There was no way that they would get to the airport on time without a potent pick-me-up.

"I do love the French brew coffee we have back home, but man, this Italian coffee tastes good," Kennedy hummed, taking a sip.

"We can pick some up at the airport, and then you can get one of your fancy new gadgets to add more to our shopping list when we get home," Jane smiled as she packed her suitcase.

Kennedy nodded with a smile; she had picked up a few new AI gadgets on their trip and was already planning how to use them.

"But if we are ever going to get home, you better start packing before we miss our flight and have to spend the next two weeks living at the airport waiting for a flight home," Jane joked.

Kennedy started throwing clothes into their suitcases randomly, hoping to get it done as quickly as possible. Jane worried that Kennedy seemed anxious.

"How are you feeling about the New Year's Ball tonight?" Jane looked at Kennedy intently. They hadn't had much time to talk about it.

"I don't know, honestly. I don't think it could be any worse than the Halloween party," she chuckled.

"You're right about that," Jane cracked a huge grin, glad to see that Kennedy was in good spirits. "Arthur said he wants to meet us at the airport around eight sharp."

"Okay," Kennedy started. "Just a few more moments alone," Kennedy slinked across the room, wrapping her arms around her wife's waist, hugging her from behind, resting her chin on Jane's shoulder.

"Our mornings together have been so short lately. And soon, I will have to share you with a little one. Until then, I want to soak up as much time alone with you as possible," Kennedy kissed Jane's cheek softly.

"We haven't even started looking at options yet," Jane laughed.

"I know, but I can feel it's going to happen soon."

Jane looked at Kennedy just in time to catch a pout.

"Okay, five more minutes. Then we have to get out of here."

Jane and Kennedy lay on the bed, fully dressed and packed, and closed their eyes, enjoying each other's company for a moment longer. When Jane opened her eyes again, the clock said seven-thirty. They had laid down for longer than they had meant to, and had to get out of there, stat.

Grabbing their suitcases, they headed out of the room and down to the hotel lobby to check out.

———

"There he is, Kennedy," Jane tugged on Kennedy's arm. Arthur was holding a tray of three coffees ahead of them. The airport was indeed packed. Everyone was trying to get home after their New Year's Eve celebrations.

"Here you are! I was worried you two would sleep in," Arthur handed the girls their coffees. Jane and Kennedy giggled.

"We almost did. Kennedy wouldn't wake up!" Jane winked.

After a little small talk, the group headed through the airport. They collected the tickets they purchased the night before online and headed to check in the luggage and stroll through customs.

The line was longer than they had expected. It was too bad that they hadn't had the foresight to book a return flight. Returning the stolen Medici jewellery was the only thing that they had considered when they decided to go to Italy in the first place.

They had a lot of fun in Italy. The museum they visited was incredible, making Jane and Kennedy want to learn more about Europe and European history.

"Can I have the window seat this time, guys?" Jane pleaded. She loved watching the buildings turn into blobs. And when the plane was high enough, you see the tops of the clouds underneath them.

"Yes, babe. Of course, you can," Kennedy said, wrapping her arms around Jane's shoulder and pulling her in tight. "Anything for you," she winked.

They had just enough time to grab some breakfast. It was a good thing, too, as Kennedy's stomach growled loudly. Wandering through the duty-free area, Jane picked up a few bags of dark roast coffee beans for Kennedy; Arthur was not engaging in the shopping experience, so he settled down with his book, waiting patiently. Kennedy stumbled upon a small pushcart selling fresh pastries. The smell of Canoli filled her nostrils, making her mouth water.

"Oh my god," Kennedy muttered. "I need to eat one, and I need to eat one right now."

Kennedy bought a few, sitting down to share them with the group while they waited to board their flight.

"I hope you know that you deserve the world, Kennedy," Jane smiled and stared into Kennedy's deep brown eyes.

"What makes you say that?"

"I love you so much. I cherish every day we spend together. I just wanted you to know how much I care for you." Jane wrapped her arm around Kennedy's shoulders and pulled her in for a quick kiss.

Arthur rolled his eyes at the public display of affection but smiled to himself behind his book. Suddenly, a loud beep sounded in the lounge, and a feminine Italian voice spoke shortly after the spokesperson reiterated the message in English and a few other languages.

"I guess it's time to board. Let's get this show on the road!" Jane cheered, excited to be on her way back home.

Lost in translation, none of the group realised their seats were separated. Jane had been looking forward to the window seat only to find that she and Kennedy had booked aisle seats, separated by a stranger. And Arthur was sitting right at the back of the plane. But at least they were heading home. Kennedy and Jane convinced the man in the middle seat to swap places so that they could sit next to each other. They had a smooth but exhausting flight home.

CHAPTER 2
A MIDNIGHT INTRUSION

"WHERE DID you put our clothes for tonight?" Kennedy asked Jane. The ball was starting in a few hours, and they needed to get ready.

"In the wardrobe. I'll go get everything," Jane smiled. She loved doing small things for Kennedy. She worked so hard, whether working with her programming clients or sleuthing. She deserved to be taken care of sometimes.

Jane was a stay-at-home wife. She had given up her career after they married with plans of starting a family. But life had other plans, and their dream to start a family had been put on hold, for reasons neither could remember. Perhaps that's why Jane shopped as much as she did – to fill the hole in her heart and the time she thought she would have been caring for a little one. As such, Jane also spent a lot of time baking and reading. She loved to sleuth, too, and their favourite pastime was watching mystery series on TV.

Jane brought their outfits out of their bedroom into the living room. Jane opened her garment bag first and removed a beautiful floor-length dress. With a sweetheart neckline, the dress shone with silver and sparkles all over.

"Wow. I'm speechless," Kennedy said. "That dress is going to look amazing on you."

Jane blushed and pulled out Kennedy's outfit. First, was a navy-blue dress that would hit the mid-thigh area and hug her body. The second piece of the outfit was a silver sequinned blazer.

"Wow, that is... interesting. Are you sure I should wear that?" Kennedy asked.

Jane's face fell, she knew it wasn't ideal, but she tried her best to find something Kennedy would feel comfortable in.

"I was hoping we could wear matching outfits. See?" Jane pointed to the dress and the blazer, which reflected the light in every direction. "And they're festive. Everyone knows you wear sparkles on New Year's." Kennedy smiled at Jane. Her happiness was infectious.

"The blazer isn't the issue, babe," she shook her head. "Why the dress?"

"Oh, that. Well, I bought them last minute. And online. My options were pretty limited. It was either this or a cheetah print mini dress. I thought this was the safer option."

Kennedy burst out laughing at the idea of her wearing a cheetah print mini dress. She would indeed be the talk of the party.

"Okay, let's get dressed then. We'll meet Arthur there!"

––––––––

When Jane and Kennedy arrived at the New Year's Ball, they weren't surprised that the mayor had pulled out all the stops. It seemed to be the mayor's thing, putting on an extravagant ball.

The walkway to the double doors was lined with gold carpeting instead of red this time, and the attendees were unmasked. No costumes. Everyone could see who was there.

The paparazzi were having a field day. So many celebrities, sports stars, and influential figures were mingling and chatting. Some of them even did the paparazzi a kindness and posed for photos. The mayor spared no expense and hired someone to do her own version of a "glam cam" that took videos of celebrities in slow motion.

"Hello, Mrs and Mrs Daniels," a voice whispered behind them. Kennedy whipped her head around. After the last party, she wasn't taking any chances and had her senses on high alert.

"Just me!" Arthur winked.

"Not funny, Arthur," Kennedy frowned, poking him on the arm.

Arthur was a great friend and a fantastic detective, but sometimes he could be slightly daft. Kennedy had almost been murdered at the last ball held on the premises, so it wasn't the best place to poke some fun.

"Sorry, sorry," he paused. "Also, I'm sorry I missed you at the airport after we landed, it was so crowded, and I needed to get home to get ready."

"No worries, Arthur; how was your flight?" Kennedy asked.

Kennedy wasn't actually expecting a response. Arthur wasn't usually the type to talk about monotonous details. He typically had a purpose behind his words.

"Fun, actually," Arthur replied with a mischievous grin.

The girls exchanged a look, grinning. What had happened?

"Care to elaborate?" Jane asked.

Kennedy and Jane waited expectantly. Even though celebrities surrounded them, Arthur had clearly met someone very important. Jane and Kennedy had very different types of people they looked up to. Jane admired many women on the cooking channel, and Kennedy fancied people who were super intelligent and worked with AI and other technology. Arthur blushed before responding.

"My ex-flatmate, Mary, was on the plane. She was in the seat right next to me, spent her Christmas visiting her son. It was a blast from the past. I think I may have told you about her before," Arthur looked between Jane and Kennedy, who looked back blankly.

"Apparently not. Anyway, she was my flatmate after I graduated from university, she is a nurse now. Her skills proved very handy after a few rough nights out...." Arthur trailed off, seeing the grins on Kennedy and Jane's faces.

They had never seen Arthur so excited. Looking back, they couldn't remember him showing much interest in any woman or having a relationship while they had known him.

"I'm sorry, I'm rambling; let's go inside," Arthur blushed.

Jane, Kennedy, and Arthur walked up the steps and entered the grand building. Sparkly decorations hung from every wall, and a giant disco ball hung from the ceiling. It reflected light in every direction as it spun. It was stunning, awe-inspiring.

The tables below had beautiful crystal centrepieces, and there were flecks of glitter all over the place; even the silverware was sparkling. Somehow, the whole building smelled of sweet champagne. It was intoxicating.

"Wow, the mayor has outdone herself this time!" Jane smiled.

She started walking down the stairs, still admiring the beautiful decorations. The music could be heard more clearly, now, and an Ariana Grande song was playing. Jane turned her head around to ensure Kennedy was walking right behind her and suddenly felt her foot slip off the polished steps. She landed at the bottom of the stairs with a loud thud, and her world faded to black.

CHAPTER 3
THE BILLIONAIRE NEXT DOOR

BEEP, *beep, beep.* Jane groaned. Was her alarm going off already? She didn't remember anything from the night before. She didn't even remember whether she had been drinking or not. Jane tried to stretch out her hand to reach for Kennedy, and a sharp pain shot through her arm.

She groaned even louder. *What's going on?*

Slowly opening her eyes, Jane was greeted by a bright fluorescent light. It stung a little, and she quickly closed them. *Am I dead? Is this the white light?*

"Jane, are you awake?" A shoulder touched her arm softly. Jane would know that touch anywhere. It was Kennedy. A smile crossed her face as she attempted to nod.

"Where am I?" Jane croaked.

"You are in hospital. You fell down the stairs at the mayor's ball," she said softly. "You're going to be okay, but you passed out. You have a broken leg. Do you remember anything?"

Jane closed her eyes, trying to remember but couldn't. Slowly, she shook her head, only to be left feeling dizzy by the motion. Jane tried opening her eyes again. She wanted to know more about what happened. She was clumsy, sure, but enough to break her leg falling down some stairs? Her vision started to clear, and she could make out the outline of Kennedy.

"Hi," she croaked, cracking a small smile, "I'm good."

Kennedy laughed and smiled, brushing Jane's tangled brown hair off her face.

"You had to have surgery to reset the bone you broke. Are you in pain?"

Jane shook her head gently. The IV in her arm was pumping enough painkillers to mask the pain from her leg.

"No, I am a little groggy, I ache a little, but nothing I can't handle. I am thirsty, though. Can I have some water?" Jane asked.

Without hesitation, Kennedy was up on her feet, grabbing Jane a cold glass of water. Helping Jane sit up, she gave her a drink before settling down next to her. It was quiet, apart from the rhythmic beeps of the machines in the room. Kennedy moved closer to the bed Jane was lying on and sat down softly. She grabbed Jane's hand and looked into her beautiful blue eyes.

"Gosh, I was so worried about you. The floor wasn't even that slippery," Kennedy chuckled. "My clumsy wife strikes again."

A nurse hurried into the room to check Jane's charts. She mumbled to herself and nodded before offering Kennedy a small, almost awkward smile.

"Thanks, Mary," Kennedy grinned as the nurse hurried to her next patient.

Jane smiled when something clicked. Kennedy had called the nurse Mary, and Arthur had recently run into his ex-flatmate, Mary, who was a nurse, on his return flight to London.

"Is my nurse Arthur's roommate?"

"Yes, she's not as fun as Arthur described, though. Strictly business," Kennedy chuckled.

Usually, Arthur had a pretty good read on people. If they knew each other well, it was strange that she would be that different from his description. But it had been a long time since they had last seen each other.

Suddenly, a commotion from the nurse's station just a little down the hall alerted Jane and Kennedy to a new arrival to the ward. Jane's face lit up; that fuss could only mean one person. The door flung open.

"Jane! Oh, just look at you! You poor thing," Jane's mum stood at the door with a gift basket.

She frowned and looked around the room. "Thank goodness you're okay. I came as soon as I heard what happened."

Jane grinned at her mum. They were so close when she was growing up, and she was one of her best friends. When Kennedy and Jane married, they grew apart a little, but their bond was still strong. Her mom walked over to her bedside cautiously.

"Hi Kennedy, it's so good to see you," she said, bending down to hug Kennedy, who briefly hugged her back.

Her mother was delighted with Jane's choice to marry Kennedy. Of all the women she could have chosen, Kennedy treated her like a queen in a way that no other woman could. She was compassionate and loving and, most importantly, made Jane happy. A parent couldn't ask for a better daughter-in-law.

"Do you mind giving us a moment?" she smiled sweetly.

"Sure, I'll go get some tea. Would you like one?" Kennedy asked.

"Please," Jane's mother replied with a sweet smile.

Jane looked up at her mother. They looked similar, other than her mother's dyed blonde hair. It suited her so well, but Jane had tried blonde once, and she definitely couldn't pull it off.

"How are you, really?" her mother asked, a look of worry and concern painting her face.

It was a mother's job to worry about her daughter. Jane's heart sank in her chest. She so desperately wanted a child that she could be concerned about. After breaking her leg, it became more apparent that a child was the missing piece in her life. Laying around all morning had offered her a lot of time to think about her life.

"I'll be okay. I'm just tired," Jane yawned.

She would love to go back to sleep. Her experience in the hospital had been relatively uneventful, but regardless, she was exhausted. The pain in her leg was bothering her, and being woken up by nurses at all hours of the night was disorienting. As she was about to open her mouth, her mum interrupted.

"Get some rest. I'll check in on you later. I don't want to get in the way of your recovery," she leaned down, kissed Jane on the forehead, and left the room.

"Leaving so soon?" Kennedy asked, surprised when she returned with the teas.

"Jane's going to get some rest."

"Oh well, in that case, I'll take you home," Kennedy smiled.

Kennedy wished Jane a good night, placing several soft kisses on her forehead and allowing her time to rest. Jane felt better knowing Kennedy was accompanying her mother home; she didn't like the idea of her mother travelling around London alone at that time of evening.

That night, Jane drifted in and out of sleep. She had a dream that there was shouting in the hospital and a huge commotion; it was a vivid dream. It had felt almost real. But by morning, it was hazy.

—————

The following day, Jane woke still feeling sleepy after a night of fitful sleep. It wasn't long before Mary came in to deliver her meds. Jane's stomach growled loudly. She couldn't remember the last time she had eaten and was famished.

Mary handed Jane her meds and checked her vitals. She worked silently, her face serious. Jane wanted to get to know Arthur's friend better but could tell she was strictly business, as Kennedy had described her.

An orderly arrived with a trolly carrying breakfast. A small pot of tea with a jug of milk and sugar, fresh orange juice, scrambled eggs, and a slice of whole meal toast. Jane was salivating at the thought of eating a hot meal, even if it was hospital quality.

"How are you feeling? Did you get a good night's rest?" asked the orderly.

"I had a strange dream," Jane started.

"That is expected after sedation and the painkillers you are on," Mary said plainly.

"It felt so real. I could swear I heard a couple arguing in the room next to me. I even felt like I woke up ready to yell for them to be quiet, but I'm not sure," Jane said, sipping her juice.

Mary and the orderly exchanged an awkward glance, and the orderly hurried out of the room, leaving Mary and Jane alone.

"It was just a dream. There is no one in the room next to you. It is closed for the next few days while it is sanitised," Mary stated.

Jane nodded and continued to eat her breakfast. The more the sedation wore off, the clearer her mind became. She concentrated, trying to piece together what was real and what was not. Hospitals were usually quiet places except for emergencies, but she was sure now that it wasn't a dream.

"It wasn't a dream. I remember. I heard arguing," Jane said, a little panicked.

Mary's face stayed expressionless.

"Your vitals are fine. I shall leave you to rest," Mary said, beginning to leave. Mary stopped at the door turning back to look Jane in the eye, "I assure you, Mrs Daniels, no one is using that room for a few more days. Delusion after sedation is perfectly normal, do not stress about it."

And with that, Mary left Jane alone.

———

When Kennedy arrived later that morning, Jane was eager to discuss what she had heard. The more she thought about it, the more she knew in her heart it was not a dream, and she wanted someone to listen to her.

"I know Mary said no one was in that room, but Kennedy, I know what I heard. Yes, I may have confused it as a dream before. But my mind is clear. I heard a man and a woman arguing," Jane insisted.

Kennedy sat on the edge of Jane's bed, taking her hand and stroking it gently.

"Okay, baby, I believe you. No need to get overly excited. Mary finished her shift shortly before your mother and I left, and we saw her leaving. She wouldn't be aware of anything that happened next door," Kennedy assured her.

Jane took in Kennedy's words and nodded along. Then, a thought occurred to her; butterflies rushed in her stomach at the thought.

"What we need to do is get a look in that room," Jane chirped, attempting to get out of bed.

"Oh sweetie, calm down," Kennedy chuckled, helping Jane back into bed. "Ever the budding detective."

"Kennedy...."

"Jane, what you heard was probably a doctor and nurse arguing about a patient. You are in a hospital. After all, it can happen. Or even two worried parents taking their anxiety out on each other. Nothing to worry about."

CHAPTER 4
NURSES AND KNOTS

WHEN KENNEDY GOT HOME that night, she couldn't get her conversation with Jane out of her head. Jane had been so insistent about what she had heard. She might not have heard the words of the exchange, but Jane knew something was amiss. Kennedy couldn't put her figure on it but knew she couldn't leave it to rest. Picking up her phone, she dialled Arthur's number.

"Evening Kennedy, how can I help you?" Arthur asked.

"Hi Arthur, can you come round? I want to discuss something with you."

"I'm on my way," Arthur said, ending the call.

Fifteen minutes later, Arthur arrived. Kennedy had a pot of tea and a store-bought Victoria sponge ready and waiting. The cake wasn't nearly as nice as anything Jane could make, but it would do the job for this conversation. Kennedy reiterated what Jane had insisted on to Arthur, who listened intently.

"You know, Kennedy, without it being called in, we can't venture into the hospital room. We have no authority there."

"I know, but maybe if we got a look into the room, it might help us, even if it is nothing. It would at least ease Jane's mind and let her get some rest," Kennedy insisted.

Arthur checked his watch. Mary would still be on shift. He could venture to the hospital and pretend to be checking in on Jane, and perhaps Mary would allow him a peek inside. Arthur agreed to look into it further and headed to the hospital.

———

The next day, Jane woke with an unsettling feeling in her stomach. She hadn't been able to get the arguing out of her head, and it frustrated her that she was powerless even to take a peek. What if something had happened and someone lay dead in the next room? What if she was overthinking things out of boredom? Jane felt like she was going crazy.

"So, Jane, how are you doing? Sorry I couldn't get here sooner," Arthur smiled, bringing in a small bouquet of flowers for her bedside table.

"These are beautiful, thank you, Arthur; I'm doing better than I was the other day," Jane smiled.

Arthur sat beside the bed and waited for Kennedy to join him. When the door was closed, Jane's eyes bounced between them. Her skin itched as it did when she was about to be dragged into another case. Excitement pooled in her stomach.

"What's going on?" she asked.

"Kennedy told me what you heard the other night. She was adamant that you wouldn't settle until we looked into it further. But of course, we couldn't do that without cause," Arthur began.

Jane's pulse raced as her eyes danced between Kennedy and Arthur. Kennedy looked exhausted, like she hadn't slept at all. And on closer inspection, so did Arthur.

"I came by last night on the pretence that I was stopping by for a visit. I ventured into the wrong room by mistake. It was then that Mary found me, and I informed her of my findings. She called it in so I could be here on official police business," Arthur said.

"So, what did you find?" Jane asked, sitting up a little taller.

"The room was previously used by a man named Albert Gladstone, or at least that's what the records show. When I did some digging, we could find nothing on the man. Except the name was very similar to an alias used by a man once a bodyguard for a billionaire," Kennedy said.

"Yes, so we looked into his employer and found he had been reported missing three days ago," Arthur finished.

Jane waited patiently for them to continue. They were being vague, perhaps worried about protocol, but if something had happened, technically speaking, she was a witness.

"Have you ever heard of Mr Albert Candlestone?" Arthur asked.

Jane nodded. Of course, she had heard Albert Candlestone; who hadn't? He was one of the wealthiest men alive and had created a vast empire in the robotics industry. Kennedy looked up to him and thought he was a true innovator who deserved a good reputation and financial success. Kennedy had hoped to meet him one day.

"He's the billionaire that's gone missing. We're trying to track him down. Kennedy and I were up all-night hacking into systems, trying to figure out if any of his devices have pinged, but everything is so well encrypted that we haven't made much progress," he paused, and his face scrunched. "Any progress, really."

Jane knew how skilled Kennedy was at this sort of thing. She had managed to hack into systems previously thought unhackable. So, if she struggled with this, Jane knew how frustrated Kennedy would be. With the missing man being a personal hero of Kennedy's, Jane worried for her wife all the more.

Jane looked over at Kennedy. She looked exhausted, with bags under her eyes. All-nighters are expected when investigating cases, but Jane typically was around to make breakfast, encourage Kennedy to take naps, and care for her. This time, she had been alone. Guilt stabbed Jane. If only she had been looking where she was going, but then again, if she hadn't been in that hospital room, they wouldn't be looking into a missing billionaire—everything happens for a reason.

"Any theories as to what happened?" Jane asked.

Arthur shook his head. "None."

Though sad for Kennedy and Arthur that their all-nighter didn't amount to any leads, Jane got excited. This was her time to shine. She lived to find the missing piece of the puzzle. It was just the pick-me-up she needed. She loved sleuthing, and though she hadn't talked to Arthur yet, she had decided to get her licence to be a private investigator in the New Year. She had thought about it for a while, wanting to give her life more purpose than simply shopping and baking. It had been the plan before she had discussed starting a family, and her plan hadn't changed.

Kennedy and Jane were relatively well off but not rich. Comfortable. Having a child would make money tighter, so they would have a bigger safety net if Jane could work and put some money aside. That was the argument she had prepared for Kennedy should the need arise.

"I'll fill you in on what we have so far," Kennedy told Jane all the case details.

Mr Candlestone was in London on a business trip. A new technological advancement in biotic limbs for wounded soldiers. An advancement that was making waves for good reasons and bad. It would be life-changing for those who benefited, but other companies were working on similar things. Albert Candlestone had simply got there first, putting others' lifelong work on the scrap heap.

No one had seen him for days. He was considered to be a missing person at that point. When a comprehensive search with his tech team back had turned up empty, that's when they tried his devices, but even his wearable tech watch had turned up empty. It was as if the man had vanished.

They'd also searched databases for arrests, hospital records, and parking tickets with no luck.

"Have you checked the hospital databases? I mean, I'm in a hospital. If you were trying to find me, my name would appear in the system, right? You said the room next to me was used with the alias of one of his ex-employees. Why not search under former and current employee names and their aliases?"

"That's a lot of names Jane," Kennedy offered gently, she knew Jane wanted to help, but Kennedy was too exhausted to do an intense search.

"Wait, I remember reading an article about him once. He

commented that he once booked a hotel under his ex-wife's name to avoid the paparazzi. Try searching her name too," Jane chirped.

"I remember that article, good catch," Kennedy grinned.

Arthur nodded, taking his notepad from his coat pocket and jotting down his notes as he left the room.

CHAPTER 5
A POISONOUS PATTERN

ARTHUR WALKED DOWN THE HALL, still fervently looking at his notepad and writing. As he was about to write the last line of his thoughts, he bumped into someone.

"I'm so sorry about that," he looked up and was surprised to see yet another old friend.

"Daniella Fitzpatrick? Is that you?"

The woman nodded and smiled.

"It's Dr Fitzpatrick, now. But, you can still call me Dannie."

Arthur smiled in return. How bizarre that he had run into Dannie, too, his ex-girlfriend, from when he was in university. What were the chances of bumping into Mary on the plane and now Dannie in the hospital? For a second, Arthur thought divine forces were trying to send him a message.

"So, you ended up getting into medical school? I told you all that worrying over the UCAT was for nothing! I bet you killed it," Arthur grinned.

"Interesting choice of words Mr Detective Inspector," Dannie laughed.

They had parted amicably, and there were no hard feelings. Arthur had wanted to pursue his passion. And Dannie had wanted to pursue her dream of becoming a doctor. Now that they had both achieved their dreams, Arthur knew that they had made the right decision to split up. Too many things could have gone wrong if they had tried to stay together. Who knew they would end up meeting again like this? Perhaps it was a sign.

Dannie extended her arms out for a hug and pulled him in tightly.

"It's so good to see you, Arthur. Why are you in the hospital? Everything okay?" she looked concerned.

Of course, she would assume he was in the hospital due to an injury. He looked exhausted from the all-nighter sleuthing with Kennedy. Arthur told Dannie about Jane's tumble down the stairs at the New Year's Ball, and Dannie offered her sympathy.

"Why don't we meet for coffee later? I have to do some things for work, which is relatively time-sensitive."

"Of course, Arthur," Dannie nodded. "Come find me later in my office in the basement. Room 189, right next to the morgue. You can't miss it."

Arthur bid Dannie a farewell and continued walking down the hall. Things kept getting stranger for him. Something was off, but Arthur put it down to the nostalgia from meeting old friends as his memories flooded back to happier times.

———

Kennedy had brought a pack of playing cards with her to try and give Jane something else to focus her mind on. But no matter how many times Jane won at Go Fish or Snap, she insisted on prying for as much information as possible about Mr Candlestone. She wanted to know where he was last seen, with whom he was last seen, and any other clue that could help find him.

"Jane, please," Kennedy sighed. "I've told you everything I know. Let's take some time and sit here, the two of us, and enjoy each other's company. I feel this case is bigger than just a missing person case."

Jane tugged at Kennedy's arm and scooted over in the small bed, making room for her wife to lay down. Kennedy got into the bed and snuggled up against Jane. There was no place she would rather be. Jane had missed feeling Kennedy beside her and absentmindedly stroked Kennedy's hair, entwining her fingers in Kennedy's curls.

"I want to talk about something," Jane whispered.

"What about?" Kennedy yawned.

"When I talked to my mum yesterday, I realised just how badly I want to have a child with you," a tear dripped down her face.

Kennedy looked up at Jane, wiping away her tears and pulling her close for a tight embrace.

"We tried a donor before, and it didn't work, perhaps looking into IVF might be an option. I know it would be pricey, but you can't put a price on a child. And we could even use the same donor," Jane continued.

"He was a good donor. Great family history, a long line of highly educated relatives. Tall, dark, handsome, and those blue eyes. I still remember them," Kennedy grinned, her own excitement growing at the idea.

"When can we start?" Jane asked.

"Let's get you discharged from here first. We can start looking into IVF as soon as possible. But it's still going to take time, and I need you at full health," Kennedy grinned, giving Jane a gentle kiss.

The two lay in silence for a few minutes, simply wrapped in each other's arms. Jane imagined her life with a child. An image flashed in her mind, a little boy with ringlets like Kennedy and a little girl with blue eyes like herself. She wasn't fussed if it was a girl or boy, as long as it was happy and healthy. She would paint the nursery grey, neutral enough to work with a boy or a girl, maybe do some yellow accents. They would have to move Kennedy's office space out of the second bedroom, though, and she had no idea where all her equipment would go.

Kennedy was thinking about how Jane would make such a wonderful mum. She was compassionate, caring, and nurturing – a born mother. There was nobody she'd ever consider having a child with except for her. Kennedy imagined building new gadgets with her son, flying a drone with a daughter, and raising her to be intelligent and strong like her.

"As soon as possible," Kennedy hummed, smiling to herself.

"Okay," Jane exhaled deeply, content with her daydreams. "I love you."

"I love you more," Kennedy sighed contentedly.

———

Jane and Kennedy fell into a deep, peaceful sleep. Jane was still recovering from surgery, and Kennedy was exhausted from her all-nighter. With no leads, it was the perfect time to snuggle up and catch up on much-needed sleep.

The door slamming open woke the girls with a start. Arthur burst into the room with a determined, wild look on his face. Jane and Kennedy knew that look all too well. It was the look he got when he had discovered something and was trying to figure out the details of a case. He was oblivious to the world around him when he had that look. Case in point, he hadn't noticed that they had been sleeping.

"Jane, you were right," Arthur babbled that his words were almost squished into one. "He had booked everything in his ex-wife's name. The hotel, the conference hall, and when he was brought in, he was also booked in under her name. How they got away with that, I will never know. I guess his assistant paid off the administration staff. He's right here, in The Royal London Hospital," Arthur gushed, pacing the small room.

The news was huge; it meant the case was solved. They had found the missing billionaire, or had they? Something was still off. Arthur wouldn't have burst in so wildly if it were an open and shut case. Jane's gut twisted.

"Great, what's the hurry about, then? You found him," Jane could see the wheels in Arthur's head spinning.

Like Kennedy had theorised before, whatever was going on was much bigger than a missing person case. Was he in intensive care? Had someone tried to kill him? So many questions span in Jane's mind.

"He's in the morgue."

"What? He's dead?" Kennedy gasped.

A chance to meet her hero, to be involved in finding and saving him, ripped from her grasp. Jane could see the hurt in Kennedy's eyes, and she pulled her close.

CHAPTER 6
THE TECH TRAIL

A DEAD BILLIONAIRE in the same hospital Jane was staying in. This was incredible, almost unbelievable news. Kennedy hoped that they were the only ones to have figured this out. Once this story broke on the news, every amateur sleuth would be begging to help solve it. And the hospital would be swarming with paparazzi.

"What do we do?" Kennedy asked wide-eyed, still in shock. Her hero was dead.

"I'm going to pay a visit to my old friend, Dr Fitzpatrick. Care to join me, Kennedy?" Arthur looked over to Jane and frowned. "Sorry, Jane, but you're on bed rest."

Kennedy looked to Jane for guidance, and Jane smiled sweetly back at her, stroking her cheek. Kennedy nodded; she wanted to know what happened more than anything. She kissed Jane and left the room with Arthur.

"So, who is Dr Fitzpatrick? Another ex-roommate?" Kennedy asked, walking quickly, trying to keep up with Arthur.

Kennedy wasn't usually one for idle gossip but found she was pleased for any distraction at that moment.

"My ex-girlfriend, actually. She works here as a doctor. Her office is next to the morgue, so it seems she's the best person to talk to."

The lift down to the bottom floor was rickety and old. It wasn't used by anyone other than the hospital staff and the deceased. It was unsettling and sent a cold chill down Kennedy's spine. As the lift approached the bottom, the air became cooler, and the smell of strong sanitation and cleaning products filled the otherwise stale air.

The lift stopped with a slight thud, and the doors opened wide. There was a short hallway where the lights flickered; the bulbs were ready to give up on life too. Three doors lined the corridor, one on each side and one at the far wall. The small size surprised Kennedy. For a hospital the size of London Hospital, Kennedy expected the morgue to span an entire floor.

Arthur looked at every door; the far door was labelled *morgue*, and the other two were Rooms 188 and 189.

"Dr Fitzpatrick is in Room 189," he walked over to the door and knocked lightly. He had calmed himself down during their trip to the basement. Good, Kennedy thought. He'll approach this with a level head.

A beautiful woman with long blonde hair answered the door and smiled, welcoming Arthur and Kennedy into her office. She greeted Arthur with a warm hug and extended her hand for a shake with Kennedy.

"I'm Dr Fitzpatrick, but please call me Dannie," she smiled warmly. "Are you Arthur's wife?"

Kennedy and Arthur burst out laughing. They were great friends, sure, but Kennedy was deeply in love with and married to Jane, and Arthur was married to his job.

"No," Arthur shook his head, still chuckling. "This is Kennedy Daniels, a great friend of mine. And happily married to her wife, Jane."

Dannie's face flushed red. It wasn't the first time one of the Daniels had been asked if they were married to Arthur. Two women being married wasn't exactly unusual, but in a heteronormative society, strangers mostly assumed that they must be married to a man.

Kennedy watched Dannie and noted a small smile at the idea of Arthur being single. Kennedy couldn't help but smile when she realised that Arthur hadn't picked up on it either.

"Sorry about that, Kennedy. Such a pleasure to meet you," she paused and turned her head to look more closely at Arthur. "I know that look. What's going on?"

"Do you have a Mrs Norma Harris in the morgue right now?" Arthur was trying to act nonchalant, but it was clear that he had trouble hiding his emotions from Dannie. She made him nervous.

Dannie nodded and looked taken aback. Mrs Norma Harris was the name on the records, but the body lying in its place was a man, and Arthur shouldn't have had access to those records. Unless something was amiss, seeing as a man with a woman's name lay dead, was the case.

"Great. Have you performed an autopsy?" he questioned.

Shaking her head, Dannie told Arthur and Kennedy about their system's problems for the last couple of hours. She wasn't authorised to work until the system security was restored. She wouldn't do an autopsy unless there was an investigation into the patient's death, and they had the man's authentic details, and a next of kin had been informed.

Arthur looked sheepishly at Dannie.

"That was me, sorry. I tried looking through the more accessible database but couldn't find what I was looking for. I hacked the system," Arthur looked at Kennedy. "Kennedy here wouldn't have left any traces, so I probably should have let her do it, in retrospect."

"No worries, Arthur. To be honest, I had a suspicion that something like this might happen. It's unheard of that a man is booked in under a name not his own. On the records, the dead body belongs to Mrs Norma Harris, but I have no idea who lays in the morgue."

Arthur and Kennedy filled in Dannie about the case. Arthur asked questions about his stay at the hospital. When was he brought in? What was he treated for? And who fudged the records to hide his identity?

After digging into the hospital records, Dannie discovered that he had been in the hospital since New Year's Day. He was brought in after he broke his wrist in the hotel he was staying at while he was in London. A slip in the shower. That's why he was in the orthopedic ward next to Jane's room. His medications seemed normal for his symptoms, and he only had two nurses and one doctor providing him care – Dr Hamilton, nurse Mary, and nurse Juliette. They guessed the staff were paid to keep their mouths shut in case the paparazzi discovered he was there.

"And what is the official cause of death?" Arthur asked.

"I haven't done an autopsy, so there isn't one. I'll take a look and see what the chart says because, as of right now, that's the most official documentation," she walked over to her desk and pulled a file from a stack. Her desk was messy, but it looked like organised chaos as she quickly found the file.

"There isn't a cause listed, though it mentions some heart issues during his stay. Other than that, there's just a time and a signature from nurse Mary."

"Aren't nurses required to write more details than that?" interjected Kennedy.

Mary was Arthur's ex-flatmate, so she was concerned that his judgement could be clouded. She was also worried that Mary was Jane's nurse. Had the nurse been doing a good job of ensuring details about Jane's recovery were being kept? Proper documentation was essential and could be a big deal if there were complications. Or was she hiding something bigger? Was Jane in danger? Kennedy needed to know.

"Yes, they are. This report is bizarre… and cause for further investigation," Dannie said, clearly annoyed.

Kennedy could see the similarities and why Arthur was taken by her. Beauty aside, she was an intelligent woman and took her job as seriously as Arthur took his.

CHAPTER 7
THE AFFAIR EXPOSED

KENNEDY LEFT Arthur and Dannie to go over more details about the case before Dannie could start the official autopsy. Kennedy wasn't a fan of blood and gore, so she chose to leave them be and fill in Jane about what they had discovered.

As she passed the room next to Jane's, yellow tape was being put over the door in the shape of an X. The investigation had officially started, and it wouldn't be long before the whole world knew about Albert's death.

"Jane, are you awake?" Kennedy opened the door slowly and poked her head in. Jane was sitting up in her bed and smiled at her.

"Yes, I can't rest without knowing more details. I have seen police officers walking past my room for hours. My mind is going crazy!" she laughed and beckoned Kennedy over to the bed.

"So, Dannie is Arthur's ex-girlfriend. Isn't that wild? I've never even thought about him dating. He loves his job too much to spend time getting to know somebody romantically."

Jane laughed and thought about how odd it would be to see Arthur with an ex-girlfriend.

"Was she beautiful? I feel like she would have to be gorgeous to catch his attention." Kennedy nodded.

"Skinny and blonde. A little stereotypical, if I'm honest."

"Enough about Arthur, now, what happened to Mr Candlestone? Is it case closed?"

Kennedy shook her head and walked over to the door to ensure it was shut tightly.

"There is some issue with the report. No autopsy was performed because there was no reason to do one; it was just a regular death. But the report that nurse Mary wrote had no details at all. There was only a time," Kennedy paused. "He was in the room next to yours. Your suspicions had been correct. If you hadn't been so insistent, we might never have found out what happened to him."

Jane's eyes widened. The shouting. Because it was still so foggy, she had no recollection of what was said and certainly wouldn't recognise the voices.

The girls brainstormed all the possible reasons for the shouting that they could. It could have been a mistress since he was so wealthy. He might have become violent to one of the staff if he was confused and overly medicated. What if Mary had witnessed the murder and been paid by the killer to keep quiet and cover it up? What if she had over-medicated him and covered it up out of fear? Or had one of his tech rivals found him and killed him?

"Hopefully, Dannie and Arthur can figure out what went wrong on the hospital side of things," Kennedy sighed.

Just then, the door swung open, and Jane's mum was standing in the door frame again. She smiled big and walked up to the girls.

"It's great to see both of you. I couldn't stay away. I had to check on my baby girl."

Jane was so thankful for her mum. It was great to see her again, and she was glad she had come a few times. She must have taken a lot of time off work. Jane chatted with her mum for a bit, but her mind was elsewhere. That is until Jane's mum brought up children.

"So, have you and Kennedy considered having children?" she smiled. "I'd love to be a grandma one day, you know."

Jane told her mum about their plans to look into IVF after failed donation attempts years ago, which halted their plans. It was too painful seeing the negative pregnancy tests month after month. They had agreed to look at other options but never had until now.

"Jane, you're going to be an amazing mum. I'm so happy for you."

A tear rolled down her mother's cheek.

———

Arthur and Dannie studied the file and figured out that Mr Candlestone's symptoms at the end of his life were more accurately aligned to poisoning. Not natural causes at all.

"We need to get a court order to do an autopsy," Arthur nodded, and Dannie agreed.

"I'll get down to the station and talk to my team. I'm sure we'll be able to get an autopsy no problem. I should be back in a few hours," Arthur paused. "If you get a free moment or two, could you check on the Daniels? They're great people, and I trust them to be of assistance in my absence."

Upon exiting the hospital, he was greeted with fresh air. The sky was a bright blue, and a few fluffy clouds floated around. The temperature was cold, but it was January, and that was to be expected. After being inside the hospital for a while, he had gotten used to the stale air. Outside, he saw Mary sitting on a bench and smoking a cigarette.

"Mary, mind if I sit with you while I wait for a taxi?" Mary patted the bench next to her.

Arthur examined her closely. Her muscles were rigid, and she had deep purple circles under her eyes. She looked as though she had been crying. The Mary he knew didn't cry unless it was really bad. She was too analytical for emotions. He wondered what had happened and if it was related to the case. He dared not think Mary of such a thing as murder, but he had to be objective.

"How are you, Mary?" he asked.

"You know, the usual. We had a patient die yesterday, which is always hard," she sighed, not making eye contact with Arthur.

Mary took another long pull of her cigarette, blowing the smoke high into the air. Arthur had never known Mary to smoke; he wondered when she started. He couldn't figure out what Mary would have to do with a billionaire. Perhaps there was a medication mistake, an accidental double dose?

He was about to open his mouth to speak when a taxi pulled up. The streets were busy, and a few people were outside also eyeing the car. Somebody would get it first if he dawdled.

"I better get that," he looked at Mary. "I'll be seeing you later."

Mary waved him off dismissively, still refusing to make eye contact. Arthur's chest constricted. Could the sweet, caring Mary he knew from time ago be involved? Could she be a killer?

———

Returning to find Jane and Kennedy asleep in Jane's bed, Arthur woke them gently. After all, he had news to share. The team got approval to make an autopsy request because Dannie had written a compelling letter stating that the report was sketchy and required an investigation.

The next step was to interrogate Mary and determine why there was a suspicious lack of details regarding Mr Candlestone's death. He still couldn't make sense of it. He had been toying around with the idea that she had forgotten to add a page to the file. If she had been on a double shift, it was possible.

"Kennedy, would you like to accompany me? We can do good cop bad cop," he looked down at his hands. "I'm not sure I can be too hard on her, and I'd appreciate your help."

Kennedy nodded. Mary walked in to take Jane's vitals as they were about to leave. Arthur turned to block Mary before she could get to Jane. Mary looked up at Arthur, surprise and horror plastered her face. Was it a sign of guilt?

"I'm going to have to ask you to come with us, Mary. We have a few questions for you," his voice was stern and firm – His detective's voice.

It wasn't harsh or meant to intimidate, just to set boundaries and ensure that she knew he wasn't talking to her as his old friend. He was talking to her as an officer of the law. Mary looked like a deer caught in the headlights.

"What is this about?" Mary stuttered.

"I think you know what this is about," Kennedy used her most intimidating voice, her eyes hard glaring Mary down.

"Follow us, please. This won't take long," Arthur added.

Arthur, Kennedy, and Mary walked through the hospital and went downstairs to Dannie's office. Kennedy loudly knocked on the door. It swung open, and Dannie stood there, looking stern.

"Come in," Dannie was the type to do everything by the book and took her job very seriously.

Knowing that she worked with a nurse who didn't care about adequately filling in reports was bad enough but knowing that one of her colleagues was suspected of poisoning a patient, let alone a billionaire, was even worse.

"Mary," she nodded curtly.

Dannie pulled a chair for her and walked around to her side of the desk. Arthur took a seat at eye level, and Kennedy stood next to him, staring down and glaring at Mary.

"Were you a nurse for a man brought in and booked under the name Mrs Norma Harris, a recently deceased patient?" Arthur asked calmly.

"Yes, I was," she nodded, not making eye contact.

"And how did he die?" Kennedy snapped.

She couldn't help herself; she had to know. And her job was to be a bad cop. She wanted to make Mary squirm. Kennedy had looked up to Mr Candlestone. He was a pioneer in the robotics industry and incredibly smart. His latest invention would make a massive difference in the lives of millions, and now he wouldn't get a chance to see it to fruition. It wasn't fair. She had hoped to meet him one day to talk about all his innovations and even share her love for him with her child.

"I don't know. He just died. I'm not a coroner."

Kennedy glared and put her hands down on the desk. "He just died?" The way she worded it was almost cruel. A man lost his life under her care; she was responsible for knowing why. And if she didn't, she was responsible for requesting an autopsy for further evaluation. Kennedy leaned forward to intimidate her and tried to make eye contact. Mary wouldn't look her in the eye, focusing on anything else in the room.

"So, he's a medical mystery? Do you know his real identity?"

Mary shook her head. She finally made eye contact with Kennedy. Her eyes were cold and malicious.

"I need to ask a few questions and take some notes, Mary. We'll be done soon. Can you tell me about your interactions with him in your own words? We want to compare everything to what you wrote in the patient's file."

When Mary was finished being questioned, Kennedy and Dannie looked at Arthur expectantly.

"Her story matches the notes. The only issue is that the story matches word for word. There's no variance. It was rehearsed," Kennedy said, frustration starting to set in.

CHAPTER 8
UNDERCOVER IN THE WARD

"GREAT NEWS, guys! I get my crutches today. I can help in the investigation!" Jane grinned.

She was so excited to be able to join in on the sleuthing. And to meet Dannie, Arthur's ex-girlfriend.

"Are you sure that you're ready?" Kennedy asked, concerned. Jane could be a little overzealous and might have overestimated her ability to use crutches.

"Yes, I'm sure," she was still smiling.

The three of them chatted for a while, and Jane decided it was time to tell Arthur about her plans to become a private investigator. She thought it might explain why she was eager to be involved in this case.

His reaction was as expected; very supportive and excited. He couldn't wait to have Jane join him and Kennedy in their investigations. Right now, Jane was helpful and offered great ideas but didn't have Arthur's detective background or her wife's technological prowess.

Arthur's phone started ringing, and the caller ID showed that it was Dannie. The autopsy must be done.

"Alright, it's time to go talk to Dannie. Let's find out what the autopsy showed."

Getting to Dannie's office proved slower with Jane in toe. She was a little uneasy on her crutches but determined not to let them hold her back and to be involved in the case.

———

"What are the results, Dannie?" Arthur cut to the chase.

"Albert Candlestone died of digoxin poisoning and from a bullet through the heart." Her face was white and scrunched up, trying to make sense of the results.

"So whoever killed him wasn't happy that the poison was taking so long and grew impatient," Arthur shook his head.

"Someone gave him an excessive dose of digoxin, which killed him relatively slowly. Maybe half an hour after ingesting the tablets. Then, the murderer decided to fire a small calibre gun into him point blank. Probably fitted with a silencer," she paused, taking in Kennedy and Arthur's faces. "Because his heart had already stopped, the blood stains were minimal and easily wiped up by the killer afterwards."

Kennedy and Arthur were in shock. Someone had gone so far as to kill Mr Candlestone. Was this a hit? Was it someone who didn't understand how digoxin worked? What could cause someone to hold so much hatred for another that they would resort to such measures?

"Do you have access to the visitor logs? Who was with him in the hour before he died?"

"Only nurse Mary, and his wife, Emily," Dannie shook her head sadly.

"I guess we need to question Emily, then. She's suspect number one at the moment. We can question Mary again, too, if we can rule Mrs Candlestone out."

CHAPTER 9
THE BETRAYAL UNVEILED

ARTHUR WENT to the precinct to share his findings with his team. They brought in Emily and questioned her, but she was clearly a sad widow with no helpful information to offer. She mostly cried and begged for them to find out who murdered him. She even blamed Mary, saying she was the worst nurse on his team. Plus, she had an alibi; CCTV put her in the hotel bar at the time of her husband's death.

Arthur and an accompanying officer entered the interrogation room where Mary had been waiting. She looked nervous and was fidgeting in her seat. She looked different when she wasn't wearing her scrubs. Her hair was pulled up into a neat high ponytail, and she wore a dark blue jumpsuit. Arthur was still in shock that she could have done something like this. She was always a sweet girl, a little wild, but had a good heart.

The room was cold and had double-sided glass, so the walls were just black. The seats and table were drilled into the ground so they couldn't be thrown, and there was a camera in the corner of the room pointed directly at Mary.

"Mary Hernandez, you're a nurse at The Royal London Hospital. How many patients have you worked with during your career?" the officer asked.

"I don't know," she shrugged.

"You're going to have to give us more details than that. A guess, even," Arthur looked at her sadly.

"A few thousand. I've been in nursing for fifteen years," she sat up a bit higher in her chair.

She was very proud of being a nurse, as healthcare professionals usually are. The only difference was that most healthcare workers weren't being investigated for the murder of one of their patients.

"And, Mary, have you ever not filled out the cause of death in a client's file before Mr Candlestone?" interjected the officer.

"No," she shook her head. "I always fill it out. I must have been tired, and I thought I would be able to write it during my next shift. By then, the file had already been given to Dr Fitzpatrick."

Mary was visibly uneasy, her knee bounced under the table, and her eyes darted around the empty room, searching for anything to focus on other than the officers in front of her. Her entire career was being questioned initially, but it was intentional. Though it was hard to drill someone about their passion and draw upon their insecurities, they wanted her to squirm so they could find out if she was the killer. The officer moved closer to her and looked her in the eyes.

"Are you familiar with the medication digoxin?" the officer asked.

"Of course I am," began Mary. "I wouldn't be much of a nurse if I didn't. It's used to treat heart conditions."

"We know you poisoned him, Mary."

Mary's eyes widened.

"We just want to know why," Arthur said.

"Did he say something to offend you?" the officer asked.

"No... it isn't like that," her eyes started to glisten, and her lips were trembling. "It wasn't Albert. It was Emily."

"Emily Candlestone, his wife?" Arthur and the officer exchanged looks. They had just spoken to Emily, and she had come across as being heartbroken and devastated. There wasn't a single word in that round of questioning that would have rung any alarm bells. They had already ruled her out of the suspect pool. "She's the one who shot him?"

"No, Arthur, that isn't what I'm saying," she was fully crying now.

"Emily is the one who offended me. I know this will come out one day, but Albert's will was changed to leave everything to me when he died."

"Bullshit, Mary. That's not true," snarled the officer. Were they expected to believe that he randomly decided to leave a nurse his entire fortune?

"It is true!" she shrieked. "I was in love with him, okay? We were in love." Mary was in full-blown hysterics, sobbing and shaking. Her whole body was rocking back and forth in the chair.

"We were having an affair. Together almost two years. I decided to break it off because I needed money, and he wouldn't give me any. I walked in on Albert and Emily arguing about how he had changed the will and knew I was running out of time. So I poisoned him."

Arthur was shocked. His old friend Mary was not who she used to be; she was a stranger to him.

"And after you poisoned him…?" the other officer wanted to figure out whether or not she was the one who shot him, too. She wouldn't have needed to shoot him if she had administered the lethal digoxin dose.

"When they were fighting, I went out for a cigarette. I saw Emily's car parked outside, and the doors were unlocked. She had a little gun in the glove box…and I took it…and shot him in the heart," she gasped. "Because he broke mine! I wouldn't have to do this if he left her."

Arthur was appalled at what he was hearing. She did murder him. He felt sick to his stomach.

"I loved him. You have to believe me," she pleaded. Arthur looked down at his hands, his heart heavy. Mary was a great friend. But he had nothing to offer her now, after what she did.

"Mary Hernandez, you're under arrest for the murder of Albert Candlestone. Whatever you do or say can and will be held against you in a court of law." Arthur grabbed Mary's arms and pulled them behind her back, clasping the cuffs on each wrist.

CHAPTER 10
A NEW YEAR'S JUSTICE

MARY'S TRIAL was lengthy and highly publicised. Given Mr Candlestone's billionaire status, it was making global headlines. The tech industry, in particular, was in chaos. His business partners pushed forward with his biotech design while others tried to fight that he had stolen their ideas. With no Mrs Candlestone to fight his case, it made for compelling court room drama.

Kennedy and Jane were mostly left out of it; the only time Jane had to testify was to confirm that she heard yelling coming from the room the night Mr Candlestone died.

Arthur and Dannie had rekindled their romance. They were practically inseparable outside of working hours. Her assistance on the case was so greatly appreciated that Arthur had decided to take her to dinner. And then they went to another dinner and another...until they officially became a couple. He was happier than the Daniels had ever seen him.

While Jane's leg finished healing, the Daniels spent most of their time at home. Kennedy had started to review the requirements for IVF and the best hospitals. Jane had begun working on her private investigator licence. A lot of it could be done online, though she had a mentor who took her on stakeouts. They were working on a case of a wealthy woman trying to catch her husband cheating. That was the most common reason for someone to hire a PI these days; not as exciting as Jane had hoped, but still, she was happy. Putting together the clues and compiling evidence gave her a rush. Solving the mystery was so satisfying to her.

A few clients had approached Kennedy to upgrade their various business and software programs, giving Kennedy some extra spending money. They decided to put money aside to take a nice romantic cruise for Valentine's Day, which was right around the corner.

Through the stress of the trial, they had spent a lot of time together and had an even stronger bond. They didn't know that was possible. Much of their time was spent talking about their child's future. More importantly, who they would look like. They had decided to use the two-egg method, where an egg from Jane and an egg from Kennedy would be used. That way, it would be a surprise and take the stress of choosing away from them.

They still had to pick which one of them was going to be pregnant. But that conversation could wait until another day. Right now, they are content with their lives and their careers. Jane wanted time to finish her licence and work to save money, and Kennedy had dreamed about visiting Japan before their future child was born.

Life was good, and it would keep getting better—a New Year, a fresh start and the fun of not knowing what the future held.

The End

POISONED ON VALENTINE'S

A COZY MYSTERY

CHAPTER 1
LOVE ON THE DOURO RIVER

IT HAD BEEN an eventful holiday period for Jane and Kennedy Daniels. Though their plans had been derailed by one thing and another, it was finally time to start a family. Unable to celebrate their wedding anniversary properly due to Jane's cast, Kennedy had booked a surprise river cruise in Portugal for Valentine's Day. Jane could hardly wait.

———

Jane was like a kid in a candy store. Every sight her eyes fell on amazed her. They began their journey in Porto, in the medieval riverside district of Riberia. The narrow, cobbled streets were lined with bright and colourful buildings; everywhere you looked were more wonders to behold. Wine merchants and cafés lined every street, and the people were so warm and welcoming to visitors. Their tour was set to take them down the beautiful scenic and tranquil Douro River. The river cruise would sail through the north of Portugal, passing miles on vineyards on top of hills and the shoreline. Kennedy had chosen this particular cruise for the relaxing peace of the enchanting city steeped in history. On the days they would dock in different ports, the options for sightseeing and shopping were endless – an aspect of the cruise Kennedy knew Jane would enjoy.

The cruise boat was a long slimline vessel of two stories. The lower deck was for dining and entertainment; the second floor was for the sleeper compartments. The top deck was lined with sun loungers and a selection of tables and chairs for everyone to enjoy the beautiful views they travelled through.

Their cabin was on the middle deck, a small cosy room fit for two. A large queen-sized bed filled the middle of the room. The opposite wall on the foot of the bed had been converted into a combination of fitted wardrobes, a dresser, and a large TV. Tea and coffee facilities were on a small table next to the floor-to-ceiling window, which gave the perfect view of the river day and night.

"Oh, Kennedy, look at this," Jane chirped, picking up the welcome packet and waiting for them on the bed.

"What is it, sweetheart?" Kennedy grinned, putting their suitcases in the wardrobes.

"Our first night will be spent docked here in Porto. There is a map exploring the city if we want to leave the ship, and tonight at dinner, the entertainment will be local dancers and historians explaining local traditions. Oooh, and a wine tasting of local wines from the vineyard," Jane exclaimed as she sat on the bed, skimming through the week's itinerary.

"How nice! What else?" Kennedy asked, joining Jane on the bed, resting her chin on her shoulder.

"Day two looks fun, a tour of the historic valleys of Guimaraes, also known as the cradle of the Portuguese nation, and day three....," Kennedy snuck in to cut Jane off with a kiss.

Kennedy already knew what the tour had in store. What Jane didn't know was that Kennedy had planned for them not to leave at the end of the week. Kennedy had found an award-winning fertility clinic to begin the next part of their journey in starting a family. The first visit was a consultation; the Daniels still had to decide which one of them would be the birth mother.

"I love seeing how excited all this makes you. Just wait until you see what surprises I have in store for us," Kennedy smiled.

"Surprises? Like what?" Jane asked excitedly.

"Now that, my love, would be telling," Kennedy winked.

Jane pouted playfully, folding her arms across her chest, making Kennedy burst out laughing. A slight tap on the door gave Kennedy a perfect break in conversation.

"Good morning! As requested, Mrs Daniels, if you need anything else, please do not hesitate to ask," smiled a well-dressed server in a white suit with a black bow tie.

"Thank you," Kennedy smiled back, handing the man a small tip before taking the bucket and tray and closing the door.

"Who was....," Jane stopped when Kennedy turned around, holding an ice bucket filled with a bottle of champagne and a small tray of chocolate-covered strawberries.

"I arranged for us to have a little treat to start our anniversary and Valentine's Day celebrations," Kennedy smiled. "Care to open that door? My hands are sort of full," Kenny nodded towards a door at the end of the wardrobe that Jane hadn't noticed.

When Jane opened the door, her mouth fell open. They had their own small private living room. Kennedy set the champagne and strawberries down on the table by the window and popped open the champagne pouring them both a glass.

"Happy anniversary, darling," Kennedy raised her glass in a toast.

"I love you so much. How did I get so lucky?" Jane smiled, a tear of joy escaping the corner of her eye.

"I was about to ask you the same thing."

———

Jane and Kennedy enjoyed their strawberries and champagne while watching Porto go by out of their window. The girls explored the cruise boat to familiarise themselves with the onboard facilities as the day drew on. Just past the three dining rooms was a small section of shops for guests to buy local trinkets and luxuries to take home as souvenirs.

"Go on, sweetie; I know you want to. I'll meet you back at the room in an hour so we can prepare for dinner," Kennedy kissed Jane on the forehead and let her wife go enjoy her shopping.

Shopping was Jane's thing, the only items Kennedy liked shopping for were new gadgets for their home, and she didn't think she would find any of those on board.

Kennedy wandered around the dining areas and the entertainment lounge before venturing to the top deck to see the stunning views from another angle. Standing on the edge of the boat, looking out over Porto as the sun set, her mind began to wander. She couldn't wait to reveal her surprise to Jane but wanted to save the announcement until the end of their trip. She wondered about taking trips like a cruise with their child one day. They could enjoy the rich history of new countries, and she could teach her future son or daughter about all the technologies she loved. Then, Kennedy pondered the idea – would she prefer a boy or a girl? Finally, she decided she didn't care. She just couldn't wait to see how Jane would take to motherhood.

Kennedy, like every first-time mother, had small doubts about her abilities as a mother. But deep down, it warmed Kennedy's heart that she had Jane by her side no matter what. Jane was a natural mother. She was born to care for others.

"Hey hon, how was the exploring?" Jane asked as she fiddled with all the things she had bought.

"Great, looks like the shopping trip went well," Kennedy laughed.

"As always, did you meet any other passengers on your trip?"

"A few said hello, mostly older couples enjoying their golden years," Kennedy answered.

"Same here; I had to laugh. I overheard two women arguing over which dining room would be better and what time to eat. They looked like sisters," Jane grinned, taking a seat on the small sofa by their living room window.

"That's cute."

"I wonder if we will ever end up arguing like that when we are old and grey," Jane pondered.

"I hope so but let's not worry about that now. I think it may be a while before we get a chance to take a trip like this for a while,"

Kennedy said, hooking her arm around Jane's shoulders and joining her on the sofa.

Kennedy mindlessly played with strands of Jane's blonde hair, entwining them around her fingers.

"Why do you say that?" Jane asked with a touch of concern in her voice.

"Well, children are expensive," Kennedy chuckled.

"That's true," Jane replied, snuggling closer to her wife.

The Daniels sat comfortably in silence in each other's arms, watching the twinkling lights of Portugal. They were so comfortable with each other. Simply sitting and being together was always so touching and tender.

"Have you ever wondered what it would be like to be pregnant? To carry a child and feel it grow inside you?" Jane wondered.

Kennedy thought on it for a while before answering.

"I can't say I have. Before I met you, I never thought about having a family. Have you?" Kennedy asked.

But Kennedy already knew the answer. Jane had been aimlessly rubbing her tummy while they sat together, and the more Kennedy thought about it, she had noticed Jane would do it a lot lately.

"I think it would be wonderful," Jane sighed.

"So, when we find the right place to start the next part of our journey to becoming a family... Would you like to be the birth mother?" Kennedy asked.

Jane practically jumped from her seat. Her face was alight with joy and hope, and her eyes sparkled like the stars outside their window with unushered tears of joy.

"Kennedy Daniels, are you asking me to carry our baby?"

"If that is what you would like to do."

"Nothing would make me happier," Jane gasped, flinging her arms around Kennedy.

Jane squeezed so tight that Kennedy struggled for air, laughing as she pushed Jane away.

"Careful," Kennedy coughed playfully, "any more hugs like that, and you will kill me."

"I wouldn't even joke about that, not with the luck we have had of late," Jane sighed, worry etching her face.

"Don't let your wonderful mind dwell on it for another second. Let's get changed for dinner; I'm starving," Kennedy said.

―――――

Dinner onboard was predicted to be a wonderful event with dancers and historians explaining the local history of the port. Most of the ship had agreed on attendance, with only a handful of guests opting to have dinner on land instead.

With it being a celebration of their anniversary, Jane had opted for a simple yet elegant low-cut black cocktail dress with a white ruched sleeve blazer and white high heels. She had spent extra time curling her hair and pinning it into a high ponytail.

"Jane, you look stunning," Kennedy gasped as she watched Jane apply a deep scarlet lipstick in the bathroom mirror.

"Thank sweetie, you look.... wow, Kennedy, you're actually wearing high heels," Jane smiled as she turned as cast her eyes on her wife.

Kennedy had opted for a black halter neck jumpsuit with a silver sequined neckline and black blazer. As someone who rarely wore anything other than sneakers or ballet pumps, Kennedy was even taller in a pair of Jane's black and white high-heeled shoes.

"Don't get used to it. It's a special occasion, and they are coming off the first chance I get. I have no idea how you always wear these," Kennedy laughed.

"I can't wait for dinner; I get to walk in with the most beautiful woman in the world," Jane said, wrapping her arms around Kennedy's neck and gently kissing her lips.

"No, you don't; I do," Kennedy replied, enveloping Jane in a loving embrace.

"Let's head to dinner before we get distracted and don't end up leaving," Kennedy winked, taking Jane's hand and leading her to the main dining hall.

Dinner was a three-course meal of Portuguese dishes. The selection was huge for such a small cruise liner. There was something for every-one, soups, pates, salads, and fruit starters, with a mix of vegetarian and vegan options. The deserts had court Kennedy's attention right away. She was glad she had two courses before to help her decide.

The dining hall was laid out beautifully with tables dressed in white and gold tablecloths with matching cream and gold studded padded chairs. Each table had a small vase filled with local wildflow-ers, and a gentleman sat on a small stage area by the bar playing the guitar.

Jane and Kennedy opted for a table by the window overlooking the river; the moonlight danced across the water. The lights from the top deck reflected a rainbow of colours across the river. The beautiful sight offered the perfect romantic setting to start their holiday.

"Excuse me, what is the Caldo Verde?" Jane asked the waitress.

Jane had been practising her Portuguese in preparation for the cruise, but she hadn't made as much progress as she would have liked.

"It is a northern Portuguese soup made of shredded kale, onion, potatoes, garlic, and chourico. It can be made vegetarian without adding the chourico," answered the beautiful olive-skinned young woman.

"That sounds delicious, Kennedy?"

"I'll have the same," Kennedy nodded.

"And for the main course?" asked the waitress.

Jane took her time deciding but thought she would go through herself into the Portuguese culture and cuisine, finally settling on Polvo a Lagareiro. Oven roasted octopus with potatoes, vegetables, and lots of olive oil. Kennedy was surprised by Jane's choice but couldn't wait to sneak a bite and try it for herself. Kennedy ordered Arroz de Pato. Jane informed Kennedy that according to her transla-tion, her dish was duck rice.

"That is correct. It is one of the most comforting dishes in all of Portugal. You will find it on every menu across the country. It's a personal favourite. I highly recommend it. The chef on board makes the best Arroz de Pato I have ever tasted," the waitress enthused.

"That's decided then; thanks for the recommendation," Kennedy smiled, her mouth watered at the thought.

"And for dessert?"

With Jane being an avid baker, the choice for her was easy. She opted for Pai de Deus, according to her Portuguese translated to God's Bread – A sweet golden bread filled with coconut. Kennedy took a bit longer to decide but finally settled on Brigaderio, a bite-sized chocolate cake sweet and rich in flavour and another recommendation from the waitress.

Between courses, the guests were entertained with music, local dancers, and storytellers hopping from table to table to explain local traditions and histories. The Daniels were enthralled with the historians. After their trip to Italy, they decided to spend more time in Europe and get to know its history. Each course offered a different wine to complement each course. Jane knew not to drink red wine; it always gave her the worse headache hangovers, but she thought one glass with dessert wouldn't hurt.

"Oh my goodness. This cake is amazing. How is yours?" Kennedy asked, hoping Jane would offer her a bite.

"I'll share mine if you share yours," Jane winked.

Taking a forkful of one of her small cakes, Kennedy leant across the table and popped the cake into Jane's mouth. Jane closed her eyes and hummed as the rich flavours took hold.

"Oh wow, the best I've ever tasted. Here try mine," Jane reciprocated the gesture.

"Outstanding; you have to make this when we get home,"

"Next time we step ashore, I have to find a bookstore to buy a Portuguese dessert cookbook," Jane chirped.

The waitress returned to the table to clear their plates, and Jane saw an opportunity to surprise and impress Kennedy.

"Obrigado pela recomendação. O jantar foi requintado," Jane said in her best Portuguese accent.

"Você é bem vindo. Seu português é excelente," smiled the waitress.

"Care to translate?" Kennedy chuckled.

"I thanked her for her recommendation and told her dinner was exquisite, and she said I was welcome, and my Portuguese is excellent," Jane beamed with pride.

"Since when have you spoken Portuguese?"

"I've been practising."

"You forever surprise me," Kennedy reached across, taking Jane's hand, stoking her knuckles with their thumb.

After dinner, Jane and Kennedy headed to the lounge where the entertainment had continued with local dancers in fabulous frilly lace and colourful dresses dancing with the guests. As the night drew on and the dancers left, Kennedy took Jane's hand and led her to the dance floor. They slowly danced together to the soft, gentle strums of the guitar player.

"I'm having such a wonderful time," Jane whispered.

"The fun is only just beginning," Kennedy replied.

CHAPTER 2
A FATAL VALENTINE

KENNEDY WOKE before Jane the following day. The river cruise had officially started, and the boat sailed peacefully down the river towards their next stop of Guimarães. Jane had mixed her drinks the night before, so Kennedy anticipated Jane would wake with a slight hangover. Kennedy ordered room service breakfast and brewed fresh coffee before heading to get her shower.

Jane woke to the delicious smell of fresh coffee and Tosta Misha, a soft bun with a crunch herb coated top stuffed with ham and cheese. Next to her on the nightstand was a bottle of water and a packet of aspirin with a note from Kennedy.

For the hangover x

Jane took two aspirin and drank the water until the bottle was empty before wrapping herself in the white fluffy dressing gown. She headed to the table next to the window. Jane watched the world go by to the soft sounds of the shower, drinking her coffee, and enjoying her food. Enjoying the view of everyone going about their day-to-day lives in the beautiful architecture spanning the shore as the scene slowly merged into hills of beautiful green spotted with wildflowers and trees before the first vineyards came into view.

"How's your head?" Kennedy asked as she towel dried her hair, emerging from the bathroom.

"Better, thanks to the aspirin and food. You are so thoughtful."

"I figured you might need them. You drank red wine and whiskey from the bar. You know you can't mix your drinks."

"I know," Jane admitted.

"So, what's on the itinerary for today?" Kennedy asked, joining Jane at the table and tucking into her breakfast of fig jam and toast.

Jane read out the notes on the welcome packet. The plan was for the guests to head ashore and explore the perfectly preserved old town with Afonso Henrique's Grand Castle. Then, after a quick tour of the city, the guests would visit the Duke's Palace of Braganza. From there, there would be entertainment on the top deck while the boat continued to sell through the Douro Valley, where the guest could enjoy the scenic views of the sleepy villages in the picturesque countryside of Regua.

"I better get ready; the itinerary says we are due to dock just after lunch," Jane said, heading to the bathroom.

———

Jane and Kennedy were the first guests to depart the boat waiting for the tour to begin. Jane's head was feeling a lot better now that she had lined her stomach, but Kennedy had packed some more aspirin and plenty of water throughout the day. Kennedy had become accustomed to Jane being the caregiver in the relationship. But the more she thought about them starting a family, the joy of being a mother seeped into her. She found she wanted to give Jane the love and devotion she had received throughout their relationship.

"Hi, are you waiting for the tour?" asked the tour guide.

"We are. When does it start?" Kennedy asked.

"As soon as the other guests arrive. We should be leaving shortly."

The tour guide was a muscular young man who obviously took great pride in his appearance. He had a Spanish accent, but Kennedy thought he was Brazilian by his dark eyes and caramel skin. While they waited for the other guests to arrive, Kennedy and Jane made small talk with the tour guide.

His name was Ramon, and he was indeed Brazilian. His great-great grandparents had moved to Portugal after marriage, and their family had loved it so much that they never left. He was studying to be a personal trainer and used the tour guide job to supplement his income.

"You seem to love your job. You speak about it with such passion," Jane said.

"I do. While fitness is where my heart lies, I've always loved history, so this was the perfect job for me until I can follow my dream," Ramon answered.

"That's beautiful and a statement I'm sure Jane can agree with. Following your dreams and family is so important," Kennedy grinned, hooking her arm around Jane's shoulders.

Shortly after, the other guests began to arrive. They were a mix of older couples enjoying retirement, friends having a break from city life, and young lovers delighting in the romance of the river. Jane and Kennedy loved people-watching and had fun figuring out the lives of each person. There was such a mix of characters and cultures. All shapes and sizes, a true blend of beauty and grace showing all the magical things the world had to behold.

"Right, ladies and gentlemen, can I have your attention, please? Now that everyone has arrived, allow me to explain how the tour will work and run through a few very quick safety instructions," Ramon raised his voice high so all could hear.

Roman explained the tour would start with a walk through the Regua countryside before joining a tour bus through local towns to Guimarães, where they would head to Afonso Henrique's Grand Castle to enjoy the history. Roman explained that they would enjoy an exclusive tour of the castle towers but not venture too close to the edge as it is a steep drop. After that, they would travel to the Duke's Palace before enjoying dinner in the local town and heading back to the boat to continue their journey to Vega de Terrón.

"It sounds so exciting," Jane exclaimed.

"It is. Now, ladies and gentlemen. I hope you have your walking shoes and plenty of water, as it is a sweltering day today. If you would like to follow me, let's go. Vamos," Ramon cheered.

———

The group began walking through the vineyards. Rows of grapes grew on the vines with plenty of people tending to them. Everyone waved happily at the visitors admiring the beauty of Portugal. As the group walked through the countryside, Ramon gave detailed descriptions of the views around them, explaining each vineyard's history and its owners. A few guests asked how the wines are made, and Ramon was all too happy to explain.

"How long will it take before we reach the tour bus?" Kennedy complained.

"What's wrong?"

"I didn't expect us to be doing so much walking, and my feet are still killing me from wearing those heels last night. I'm starting to think these sneakers were a bad choice. I really wish I had my hiking boots with me," Kennedy whispered, not wanting to disturb the group or Ramon's detailed explanation of the scenery.

"I'm sure it is not long now. Later, when we get back, I will give you a nice foot massage. How does that sound?"

"Wonderful. My beautiful wife, ever the caregiver," Kennedy grinned.

"Oh hush," Jane blushed.

Eventually, they reached the tour bus, and Kennedy was eager to nap for the hour-long journey to the Afonso Henriques castle. However, Jane was disappointed that Kennedy had missed all the beautiful scenery, so she took as many pictures as possible to show her later that evening.

Just before the castle, Ramon took the group to the Alfonso Henriques monument. Ramon took the time to explain the history of the first King of Portugal. He spoke with passion, pride, and joy, giving the guests as much information about the monument as he could.

"Afonso Henriques was also known as Afonso the Conqueror. He was believed to have been born in the castle we are about to visit. He was born around 1110 and died in 1185 in Coimbra. Afonso secured a significant victory securing Portugal's independence. He is a substantial persona in Portuguese history. Once we enter the castle, you will witness some priceless historical artefacts. So it goes without saying that I ask you not to touch anything."

Ramon continued his tour around the castle gardens and the park surrounding the lands before taking the guests inside. The medieval castle held eight towers looking out over Guimaraes, with some towers reaching as high as twenty-eight meters.

Once inside, Jane and Kennedy were in awe of the impressive and beautifully preserved banquet hall. Wooden ceilings and walls are covered in an impressive collection of portraits, tapestries, and beautiful medieval furniture. Jane wondered if they were the furnishings used by the famous king. Rich, colourful carpets lined every floor, with gorgeous porcelain vases and decorative pieces dating back to the seventeenth century. Jane and Kennedy listened intently to Ramon, soaking up all the history and imagining what it must have been like when the castle was bustling with life.

"If you would like to follow me once we look out over the city from one of the castle's many towers, I will show you the beautiful gothic San Francisco Church on the south side of the city gardens. It is one of my favourite stops on tour. It was restored in the eighteenth century and holds a truly breathtaking, elegant Renaissance fountain. But don't let me spoil the surprise," Ramon boasted as he led the group up the stone steps leading to the high towers.

"Can you imagine archers standing here waiting for a command from their king? It's fascinating," Jane awed, looking out over the city.

"Truly spectacular," Kennedy replied.

"Please, everyone, I ask you not to climb, or venture too close to the edge or go past the velvet rope. It is there for your safety. But – Mr, please!" Ramon pleaded as an over-enthused guest ignored his request and began climbing higher for a better view.

A man's scream alerted the group that their tour was over as one life ultimately met a gruesome end. The rest of their river cruise would not be the same. Ramon panicked, trying to keep the rushing crowds back as everyone ran to the side of the tower where the gentleman had slipped over the edge.

"Please, people stay back," Ramon yelled.

Jane could tell he was scared from the crazed look on his face. A guest dying on one of his tours would not be taken lightly. Also, being the only tour guide as other tourists rushed to see the spectacle, he was outnumbered and didn't know what to do.

"No! Mervin! My darling Mervin," screamed a frantic woman.

She blotted her eyes with a cotton tissue from her purse.

"What happened?" Ramon asked in a panic as more staff from the castle turned up to control the crowd.

"He was climbing for a better view and slipped over the edge. I told him not to climb, I told him. I told him," the woman cried.

Ramon and the other staff gathered the rest of the group directing them back to the tour bus to take them back to the cruise liner as Portuguese authorities arrived on the scene. The tour bus was tense on the journey back. No one seemed to know what to say, sitting quietly. The tension was so thick it could be cut with a knife.

Kennedy's mind ran wild. Something was off. Mervin was an older gentleman. What was he doing climbing? And how did he manage to climb so high as to fall? Her detective senses were tingling. Yet, as they drove back through the vineyards, all Kennedy could think of was getting to her laptop.

CHAPTER 3
THE WIDOW'S VEIL

AS SOON AS they got to their room, Kennedy ran to her suitcase and dug out her laptop from under all her clothes.

"You brought your laptop? I thought we agreed to leave work at home?" Jane asked.

"I know, but it's a good job I did. Something is off about what happened at the castle," Kennedy said, setting up on the dresser.

"What do you mean?"

"Think back to last night. We met, what was her name? We met Adaline and Mervin Hoffman in the lounge. At dinner, they seemed happy, but as soon as he asked her to dance, her entire demeanour changed. It was like she couldn't stand his touch. And let's face it, he is easily twenty-five years her senior," Kennedy began typing away. She had an idea of what she was searching for and hoped she was wrong.

While Jane and Kennedy liked a good mystery and had helped on several cases over the years, this was supposed to be a drama-free trip. They were celebrating Valentine's Day and their wedding anniversary and hopefully taking the next big step to starting their family. But if something was amiss, Jane and Kennedy were in the right place at the right time. They could find out exactly what happened.

"I mean, the age difference is very apparent, but in this day and age, it's not something unusual," Jane thought.

"I was hoping I was wrong but look at this," Kennedy spun the laptop to face Jane.

On the screen were several pictures of Adaline in a different wedding dress with a different man on her arm. Each man was considerably older than her, and all had passed. Adaline was on her fourth marriage in less than twelve years.

"What are you saying?" Jane asked, not wanting to believe it but coming to the same conclusion.

"I think she's a black widow. I don't think Mervin fell. I think she pushed him. Jane, I think we witnessed a murder."

Jane and Kennedy spent the next few hours digging deeper into Adaline's previous marriages. Her first husband died in a car crash, her second had a heart attack, and her third had a fatal stroke.

"I don't think we can say she is a black widow. Yes, it doesn't look great, but two of these are natural causes, most likely due to old age. The first, she wasn't near the crash site," Jane pondered.

"I've seen other cases of black widows where it all seemed legit. I still think we should look into it."

"If you believe there is more going on than meets the eye, I believe you. So, what shall we do next?"

"I think the first thing to look into is how Adaline would benefit from Mervin's death," Kennedy began loading another screen and typing frantically.

"Try and piece together a motive."

"Exactly."

"Then perhaps we should see how she benefited from her previous husbands' deaths too," Jane said.

———

It appeared the Portuguese police believed there was more to Mervin's accident. On arrival the previous evening, the captain had instructed all guests to stay in their rooms, and the cruise liner was ordered not to leave port until everyone had been questioned.

The morning after the accident, Jane and Kennedy sat in their living room by the window, sharing a fresh pot of tea and going over what they had found the night before. Adaline was due to inherit a substantial amount of money from Mervin. Mervin was the picture of health, so the likeliness of him passing due to illness was slim. Adaline would have to wait longer than she had with her previous marriages for his life insurance to kick in, but now she was set to get everything.

"I still can't believe it. She inherited nothing from her first marriage. Her second, she entered a prenup and wasn't in his will and she inherited a couple hundred thousand from the last marriage. But, according to what we found, she still had every penny from her last marriage. Everything was in Mervin's name. She never had to spend a penny of her own funds. And from her social media, they practically lived separate lives. She had everything," Jane sighed.

"You never know what goes on behind closed doors," Kennedy replied.

Suddenly, there was a knock on the door. Kennedy went to open it to find a tall, slender dark-haired man with a thick moustache and dark-ringed glasses.

"Good morning, Ma'am. I am Detective Pedro Gabriel. May I come in and ask you a few questions?"

"Of course, would you like some tea?" Kennedy asked, leading the detective through to the living room of their suite.

"No, thank you," Pedro grinned, sitting cross-legged on the sofa.

Detective Gabriel pulled a folder from the small satchel he was carrying and thumbed through it silently before looking back to the Daniels.

"You are Mrs and Mrs Daniels. Who is Kennedy, and who is Jane?"

The Daniels introduced themselves in turn with a smile and a wave.

"I can see from my folder here you two are acquainted with Detective Author Gottfried. Is that correct?"

The Daniels smiled and shared a glance before turning back and nodding.

"Yes, we work quite closely with him," Kennedy admitted.

"Very good. From what I had gathered so far from the other passengers, you two were close to the incident when it happened. Did you see how Mr Hoffman fell?" Detective Gabriel asked.

"I was taking photographs, so I didn't see him fall," Jane answered.

"Unfortunately, I didn't see anything either. We were close by but otherwise occupied. The last time I saw the Hoffman's, they appeared to be in a heated discussion," Kennedy admitted.

"Were they in discussion or arguing?" Jane asked, seemingly reading Pedro's mind.

"They could have been arguing."

"Did you hear what was said?" Jane asked.

Kennedy closed her eyes and thought hard. In her mind's eye, she could see the scene perfectly. Adaline seemed upset, and Mervin was furious. Finally, Adaline fell quiet and walked away. She re-joined the group a few minutes later; she no longer looked upset, as if she had put on a mask to hide her pain. The couple had shared an embrace, and Adaline had handed Mervin a bottle of water before taking a small sip herself. That's when they all ascended the stairs to the castle wall.

"I didn't hear what Adaline said, but I heard Mervin say he would never grant her a divorce," Kennedy began.

She was keeping her eyes closed and thinking harder. "Adaline left after that. She wasn't with the group when Mervin fell, not that I can remember."

"Witnesses say that she was yelling that she told him not to climb," Pedro pondered, "did you see anyone else who might have witnessed anything?"

"I saw two older ladies on the other side of the tower; they were taking a selfie," Jane said.

"Do you know their names?"

"We haven't interacted with many people on our trip, but I could recognise them if I saw them again."

Pedro pulled another folder from his satchel and handed it to Jane. Opening it, Jane gasped. The folder had pictures of every passenger with their name and room number under it. On the third page, Jane recognised the picture of the women from the tower. Mrs and Mrs Laurance were only a few doors from Jane and Kennedy's room.

"That's them," Jane pointed out.

"Thank you, Mrs Daniels. This is very helpful."

———

Detective Gabriel left the Daniels alone in their room. Jane saw him at the door. She knew Kennedy had something on her mind; she had looked troubled since she remembered what she had seen. Jane also knew something was wrong when Kennedy hadn't divulged what they had found the night before.

"What's wrong, hon?" Jane asked.

"I was so sure Adaline was guilty. On the tour bus back, I could only think about proving she had pushed him. I had completely forgotten that I saw her leave," Kennedy sighed, running her hands over her face.

"Given out history with murders around the holidays, it is understandable. Is that why you didn't mention what we found last night?"

"Yeah. You knew there was nothing to it. You punched holes in all my theories. You are becoming quite the detective yourself," Kennedy smiled, but her eyes were still sad.

Jane took Kennedy's hand and offered a consoling squeeze.

"Why do you think he did it? Why do you think he jumped?" Kennedy asked.

Suicide always distressed Kennedy. The thought of someone being in so much pain with no way out, feeling so helpless that ending their life was the only choice. It never sat well with Kennedy, and Jane knew she would need her support.

"You said you heard him say he would never grant a divorce. Perhaps he knew Adaline would leave him anyway and couldn't face it. I know we didn't know Mervin, but from what we found out and his mannerisms, he seemed like a very proud man," Jane explained.

CHAPTER 4
TOXIC REVELATIONS

JANE AND KENNEDY continued to discuss the implications of Mr Hoffman's suicide. To Kennedy, something was still off, a missing piece from the puzzle she couldn't find. It drove her crazy, knowing in her gut that there was more to it but with no leads or proof to follow up on.

"Let's just try and enjoy what's left of our trip," Jane suggested.

But their trip was about to take another unexpected turn. Not long after Detective Gabriel left did he come knocking again for assistance.

"Hello, again, detective. Please come in; we were just discussing the case ourselves," Jane said, leading him back to the living room.

"You were?" Pedro grinned.

The Daniels finally divulged what they had discovered about Adaline and Mervin. Kennedy had shared her theories, and Jane shared her ideas too. Detective Pedro Gabriel nodded, his brow furrowed, listening intently. Everything the girls said made sense, but with no leads and everything they did pointing one way, what else could they do?

"How did you find all this out so quickly?" Pedro asked.

"It's kind of what Kennedy does; she's a tech wizard," Jane smiled proudly.

"Well, ladies, I will have to ask for your assistance. Of the other witnesses, Mrs and Mrs Laurance, Lucy is very nervous and has requested a female officer. Unfortunately, the female officer I have with me doesn't speak much English, and it will take a long time to get a translator here. As you both have experience working in such matters, would you mind helping conduct an interview?" Pedro asked.

The Daniels agreed. Even if it intruded on their trip, deep down, they were happy to help. This was what they lived for, and they had a proven record of success.

———

"So, just before we leave, let me see if I have got this correctly. You believe that from what we have so far, Mr Hoffman was a jealous and possessive man. You believe that when Adaline asked for a divorce, and it became clear that Adaline was going to leave anyway, his pride drove him to suicide?" Pedro asked.

"From what we have so far, I still believe we should speak to Adaline," Kennedy answered. "I believe there is more to it. Mr Hoffman might have been a very proud man, but from what I could dig up, I don't think he was impulsive. To jump so soon after an argument seems out of character."

"Let's speak with the Laurances; they may be able to shed some light on the situation," Jane suggested.

Nodding, Detective Gabriel led the way down the hall to Mrs and Mrs Laurance's cabin. The walk to the room felt strange. There was an untouchable atmosphere on the cruise boat. The nerves of every passenger seemed to electrify the air. Jane felt the hairs on the back of her neck stand on end. While she had believed that Adaline was innocent at first, the more Kennedy insisted something was amiss, the more Jane believed her.

A tall slim brunette officer stood outside the Laurance door. She smiled at Gabriel's arrival, and they conversed a little before the officer smiled and shook both Jane and Kennedy's hands. A few moments passed with a gentle knock on the door before a short, round, gentle-looking woman opened the door.

"Mrs Laurance, this is Mrs and Mrs Daniels. May we come in?" Detective Pedro asked.

"Of course, Lucy is in the next room."

———

Lucy and Alice Laurance were sweet women in their late seventies, both with curls of soft grey hair, Alice was short and round with the look of a school headmistress. Alice was slightly taller, slim, with a long face, angular nose, and large dark-rimmed glasses that almost took over her face.

Lucy sat with a blanket wrapped around her shoulders; she had clearly been crying. The effects of witnessing someone meet such a cruel and sad end had shaken her to her core. Lucy held the look of a once proud and strong woman. Alice, from her appearance, looked soft and gentle. However, from the look Alice kept shooting, Detective Gabriel, Jane, and Kennedy knew she was a no-nonsense woman.

It warmed Jane's heart. The two older women reminded her so much of her and Kennedy. Once strong and independent, the other is so willing to do everything to care and protect. They were a sweet couple, and the Daniels wanted to make the interview as pain-free as possible.

"I mean no disrespect Detective Gabriel, but do you need to be here? My Lucy is not herself, and your presence may unsettle her more," Alice said, eyeing Pedro from head to toe.

"I assure you, Mrs Laurance, Detective Gabriel is here simply to take notes. My wife and I will be conducting the interview, and I assure you we will make this as pain-free and quick as possible," Kennedy offered softly.

"Please, call me Alice. Take a seat; I shall pour us some tea," Alice smiled slightly but kept her eyes on Pedro.

———

"Lucy, can you tell us where you were when the incident with Mr Hoffman occurred?" Jane asked.

Lucy nodded, dabbing her eyes with the edge of her blanket and mindlessly staring out at the river.

"Alice and I were standing right by him," Lucy answered, her voice barely a whisper.

"Did you see anything right before the incident?" Kennedy asked.

Lucy nodded, tears brimming her eyes, her gaze falling to her lap. Alice leant closer resting a reassuring hand on her wife's knee.

"I should have done something. I could have reached out and stopped him. Why didn't I try and stop him?" Lucy cried.

"Lucy, none of this is your fault. It is admirable that you wanted to help, but without putting yourself in danger, there was nothing you could have done," Kennedy reassured.

Lucy nodded, sitting a little taller, her eyes finally meeting Jane and Kennedy.

"He was rambling. I couldn't hear what he was saying. It sounded like a made-up language, gibberish even. His eyes were wide and crazed, then suddenly he just began to climb," Lucy answered.

Jane and Kennedy exchanged a glance. This was new information. Mr Hoffman had seemed like a well-together man. What would make him act in such a way?

"It was horrible. His jaw was wild as he spoke. Like it was swinging of its own accord. He looked right through me like I wasn't even there. Then all of a sudden, he was over the edge. I can still hear the sound of...." Lucy trailed off.

"Don't say it, darling, don't even think about it," Alice said, wrapping a still crying Lucy in her arms.

"I am so sorry, Lucy. That must have been an awful thing to witness," Jane said.

"His eyes will haunt my nightmares for the rest of my life."

Gently, Jane and Kennedy continued to question Alice and Lucy, but their story only confirmed everything that Kennedy had remembered from the day before. At the end of the day, Detective Gabriel returned to their room to thank them for their assistance, but the evidence pointed to suicide, and the case was now closed.

"It looks like poor Mr Hoffman had a mental break, and that's what made him do what he did," Pedro informed them.

The cruise liner stayed docked for an extra day before continuing its journey.

CHAPTER 5
WEB OF LIES

THE NEXT DAY the river cruise continued as usual. Kennedy was particularly excited about the excursions on the itinerary for the day. They were to visit the university town of Bega de Torreon. The tour was supposed to see the eighteenth-century Casa de Mateus Palace, but given what had happened to Mr Hoffman, that tour was cancelled. Most of the other guests decided to stay on board and enjoy the last-minute entertainment and board games arranged by the crew. A few went ashore to visit the local shops and cafés, while Kennedy and Jane decided to tour some of the universities.

It took a while for the crew to arrange a tour of the universities, but Kennedy was glad they did. Re-entering a world she loved, full of education, technology, and higher learning, was exactly what Kennedy needed to get back to herself and forget about the niggling feeling in the back of her mind that she shouldn't let the Hoffman case be closed.

The cruise liner docked overnight in Vega de Terron before continuing its trip to Salamanca and Barca D'Alva. Jane and Kennedy spent a day in the sun, touring the beautiful golden sandstone buildings and the towering cathedrals, palaces, and churches. Salamanca was beautiful. Jane took so many pictures she lost count. Later that day, the tour nipped across the border to spend the afternoon in Spain. More of the guests joined for a walking tour through the narrow cobbled streets before enjoying the magnificence of the square of Plaza Mayor before they headed back to Barca D'Alva to dock for the evening.

"That was such a wonderful day. I feel like I soaked up so much of the culture," Jane chirped, jumping on the bed.

"I think you soaked up too much sun; your nose is a little sunburnt," Kennedy teased.

"Oh no, and I didn't bring any aftersun with me."

"I'll go online and see what else is recommended for sunburn," Kennedy said, opening her laptop.

Flashing in the top left top corner was her email icon. Kennedy had informed everyone that she would be out of the office for the time being, so she worried the email might be important. Clicking the email, she recognised the name right away. Sighing deeply, she let her head drop, worried she might ruin Jane's holiday with the news.

"What's wrong?" Jane asked.

"I have an email from Detective Gabriel. He says he is sorry, but he needs our help. He wants me to call him and arrange to meet next time we dock on land. I'm sorry, sweetie, but I think our holiday is over," Kennedy sighed.

———

"I hope Pedro has something important to say. We were supposed to be touring Douro today. I was looking forward to tasting all the different wines and ports," Jane complained as she packed her suitcase.

"It's probably for the best; you know what you get like with a hang-over," Kennedy teased, trying to make light of the situation.

Jane wrinkled her nose and stuck out her tongue, making Kennedy laugh. No matter what Detective Gabriel had to say, Kennedy was determined that nothing would get in the way of her plans for Valentine's Day or the day after.

The cruise docked in Pinhoa, where Jane and Kennedy had arranged to meet Detective Gabriel at a hotel. After booking in for the next few nights and dropping off their luggage Jane and Kennedy headed downstairs to the conference room to find Detective Gabriel waiting.

"Thank you so much for coming, ladies," Pedro shook their hands in greeting. "I am so sorry to have to cut your trip short. I assure you I shall personally make it up to you both."

"We are happy to help. So, what was so urgent?" Kennedy asked, sitting down at the table.

"There was something about Lucy's account of Mervin's actions before he fell that I couldn't get out of my head. So, I ordered a toxicology report as part of the autopsy, and behold – I found something," Pedro explained, sliding a folder across the table.

Kennedy opened it, and the pair scanned over the documents. Mervin had tetrodotoxin in his system.

"What's tetrodotoxin?" Jane asked.

"It's a toxin common in some sea creatures, most commonly in the blue-ringed octopus and the puffer fish. It's a rare side effect, but visual and audio hallucinations can occur," Kennedy answered.

"Wait but isn't the puffer fish and the blue-ringed octopus commonly found in Japan?" Jane asked.

"That is right. Here in Portugal, seafood is common in a lot of our dishes. A black market for more exotic tastes is always against our laws, but unfortunately, it happens," Pedro answered.

"What's your theory?" Kennedy asked.

Pedro raised an eyebrow, silently communicating what was evident to him. He believed that Adaline had poisoned her husband.

———

A plan was put into action. Detective Gabriel had sent for Adaline to be detained immediately before she had a chance to flee the country. Jane would travel back to Porto with Detective Gabriel to interrogate Adaline while Kennedy does what Kennedy does best – Digging and finding out what no one else could.

"Are you sure you are going to be ok interrogating Adaline?" Kennedy asked.

"I'll be fine, Pedro will be there with me, and hopefully, you will be there to help soon," Jane grinned.

While nervous, Jane had been making significant progress studying for her detective licence; she was training to be a private investigator. Interrogation wasn't something she expected to cover, at least not so soon. But she had witnessed Kennedy and Arthur do it several times. Jane's mind flashed back to Boxing Day when she was interrogated concerning the jewellery theft. All she needed to do was remember – Adaline would be more nervous than her.

"Are you sure you can find the information we need?" Pedro asked.

Jane and Kennedy had explained their plan to him, but after Kennedy explained how she would track down the information she needed, the pair watched Pedro's eyes glaze over. Even after their years together, Jane occasionally reacted the same when Kennedy spoke in her technological terminology. But Jane also knew even if she didn't understand it, she knew no one was better at finding things out than Kennedy.

"You will not find anyone better for the job Pedro. I can promise you that," Jane boasted.

———

Adaline sat in the interrogation room with a look of indifference on her face. Her long blonde hair was pinned into a tight French twist, and her makeup looked like it was done by a professional. If you took her out of the situation and looked purely at her ample cheeks, almond eyes and plump lips, Adaline could have been mistaken for a model.

Leaning back in her chair without a care in the world, Adaline crossed her legs and sat examining her nails. It vexed Jane how Adaline acted like being arrested for suspected murder was such an imposition. As if her actions hadn't caused a man's premature and gruesome death.

"Mrs Hoffman…" Jane began.

"It's Le Blanc now. I have taken back my maiden name," Adaline said without looking up from her perfect manicure.

"Do you know why you are here, Mrs Le Blanc?" Jane asked.

"I have no idea. My late husband decided to kill himself, and I am being blamed for murder. Ask around, check CCTV. I was nowhere near him when he jumped. I would love to know how you think I killed him," Adaline scoffed.

Jane glanced at Pedro, who inclined his head, urging her to continue. But, instead, Jane locked her eyes on Adaline and grinned. The woman was confident and arrogant, thinking she had committed the perfect crime. Her arrogance was sickening, but Adaline didn't know who she was dealing with.

"I'm glad you should ask. How does this sound? Mervin Hoffman was a proud and jealous man, but he was also the picture of health. When he wouldn't allow you to put your name on his life insurance policy, you demanded a divorce. Mervin said no, tired of feeling like a possession and unable to move on to your next victim while still married. You poisoned him with a toxin not usually detected on a toxicology report. As a result, Mervin hallucinated and jumped from the castle wall, making it look like a suicide. The perfect crime," Jane said in her sternest voice, slamming her hand on the table when Adaline laughed and glared her down.

"It's a fun story, but you have no motive. I wasn't in his will. We had a prenup, so even if I divorced him, I wouldn't get a penny. So, what would killing him get me? How would I benefit from his death?" Adaline asked.

Pedro and Jane exchanged a glance. They had nothing. They hoped Kennedy had discovered something or Pedro would be forced to let Adaline go.

"Ha! See, you have nothing!" Adaline laughed, sitting back with the most obnoxious smirk on her face.

Jane grinned back. They might not have had anything yet, but what Jane knew was people like Adaline, who thought they were smarter than everyone else, could always be broken. Adaline's ego wouldn't allow her to be made the fool; all Jane had to do was find the kink in Adaline's armour, and Adaline would trip herself up.

CHAPTER 6
A LOVE WORTH FIGHTING FOR

THERE WAS a knock on the door, three small taps – The rhythmic signal that Kennedy had the answers they were looking for. Pedro opened the door and in walked Kennedy, followed by Ramon, the tour guide. Keeping her eyes on Adaline, Jane noticed how Adaline visibly stiffened; her eyes widened slightly. She was fighting to keep her composure, but it was only a matter of time before the truth was revealed.

"Ramon, I believe you know Adaline?" Kennedy said, gesturing for him to sit in the sea beside Adaline.

"She is a guest on the cruise, yes," Ramon answered coolly.

"Oh, I think she is more than that. Adaline, how many times have you visited Portugal?" Kennedy asked.

"This is my first time," Adaline replied.

Kennedy slammed a folder on the table, making Ramon jump and Adaline's face grimace in anger. Kennedy flipped open the folder and pulled out several records. Adaline had travelled to Spain ten times over the past year, sometimes staying for weeks at a time. There were records of her crossing the border into Portugal and booking hotels in Porto.

"Care to explain these?" Kennedy asked.

Adaline didn't look at the records. Instead, stone-faced, she stared back before her face broke into a smirk.

"Why don't you tell me what crazy theory you have? I'm sure it's entertaining," Adaline smirked.

Pulling more records and evidence from the folder, Kennedy pulled the chair and sat next to Jane. Mirroring Adaline's obnoxious energy, Kennedy continued. Sensing she was being mocked, Adaline grew tense.

"Several months ago, you were removed from Mervin's will. Why was that?" Kennedy asked.

"We had an argument. He didn't like that I spent so much time travelling with friends and said that I wouldn't be in his will until I learned my place. I have my own money, so I wasn't bothered by it. I loved my husband; I wasn't with him for the money."

"Is that why you started your affair with Ramon?" Kennedy asked.

"What?" Ramon gasped.

"You two are in this together, aren't you? Who planned this murder? Who bought the toxin?" Pedro interrupted.

"What? I'm being accused of murder?! Adaline," Ramon panicked.

"Shut up! They have nothing!" Adaline barked, folding her arms across her chest.

"How is this for nothing? You travelled to Spain with your friends and met a handsome young man named Ramon. Mervin was the richest of your husbands, so once he passed and you inherited everything, you didn't have to worry about money anymore. You could marry for love. But Mervin found out and removed you from the will, so you decided to kill him," Kennedy began.

Ramon was growing visibly more scared, but Adaline was still determined she had committed the perfect crime. Shaking her head, she chuckled.

"It's a cute story," Adaline snipped.

"Oh, I'm just getting started," Kennedy slammed a second folder on the desk.

The second folder contained all the details of the private investigator Adaline had hired to follow Mervin, including pictures of

Mervin with a woman even younger than Adaline. The following page was a detailed document, the prenup from her marriage.

"You found out Mervin was cheating and demanded a divorce. As long as you could prove he cheated and he had no proof about your affair, the prenup was null and void, meaning you could take him for everything he was worth. But he refused. So, you got Ramon here to find the toxin to kill him," Kennedy smirked.

"It was her. It was all her. She seduced me and convinced me to do it," Ramon leapt from his chair, pointing at Adaline, screaming his innocence.

"Shut up, Ramon!" barked Adaline, panicking now that her plan was falling apart.

"Don't worry, Ramon. I will get to you shortly. I will give you this, Adaline. You are one of the best black widow killers I have ever seen. If it not for the specific toxin you used, you probably would have gotten away with it."

"What do you mean?" Jane asked.

"Well, honey, let me explain. Witnesses noticed how Mervin was acting odd before he jumped. Clearly intoxicated, if it were not for those accounts, Mervin's death would have been classed as a suicide because there would have been no autopsy needed. However, his behaviour was a cause for concern, and Detective Gabriel ordered a full toxicology report. The toxin in Mervin's system, in particular, it's not found everywhere. But who else would be able to find it other than a man whose job it is to form connections and tour cities? Ramon came across a black-market trade in exotic fish, and together they poisoned Mervin," Kennedy answered.

"I feel like there is more to this," Pedro said.

"Oh yes, there is. I did a bit more digging. Mrs Le Blanc took out life insurance on all her husbands under her maiden name, benefiting from each and everyone."

Kennedy continued, pulling more reports from her folder. The first detailed how the brakes on Adaline's first husband's car had been tampered with, but it had been mistaken as an accident. Another report indicated how her second husband's heart attack was due to high insulin levels and put down to undiagnosed diabetes. Kennedy had found that Adaline had purchased extra insulin for her mother, but her mother had passed several years before she married her second husband. As Kennedy detailed evidence of how Adaline had murdered all of her husbands, she finally cracked.

"Fine, I killed Mervin. He deserved it. Taking me out of his will and then having to audacity to cheat on me. The fool wouldn't even grant me my freedom with a divorce. I told him he could keep his money for all I cared. I just wanted my freedom, but no, he wouldn't have it. I needed to escape. All I wanted was to be with Ramon," Adaline yelled.

———

With Mervin's murderers finally caught, Jane and Kennedy headed back to their hotel to enjoy their last few days in Portugal before they were due to fly home. Detective Gabriel had agreed to keep them updated on the case's progress over the following weeks.

Kennedy arranged a beautiful dinner in the Douro Valley for Valentine's Day. At the top of the city's second hill was a stunning sanctuary of Nossa Senhora Dos Remedios. Kennedy had planned a beautiful picnic watching the sunset on top of the beautifully crafted terraced hills.

In her back pocket, she had the envelope with Jane's surprise. As they enjoyed their picnic, Kennedy's heart pounded with excitement. She had no idea how she had managed to keep it a surprise for so long.

"Kennedy, this is beautiful. Thank you for such a wonderful Valentine's Day," Jane kissed Kennedy softly.

"It's not over yet; I have a surprise for you," Kennedy handed Jane the envelope.

Jane peeled open the letter, and her eyes bulged. Jane rested her hand on her chest as her jaw fell open, and tears glistened in her eyes.

"Kennedy....is this....?"

"Yes. We have an appointment set for lunchtime tomorrow. So, we are finally taking the next steps in starting our family. Who knows, this time next year, we could be celebrating the birth of our first child," Kennedy croaked, getting emotional at the thought.

"First?" Jane asked.

"I was hoping for two," Kennedy beamed.

"How is it that I keep falling deeper and deeper in love with you?" Jane asked, wrapping her arms tightly around her wife.

All her dreams were coming true. Jane had a loving wife, a job she loved, a home, and soon a family of her own.

———

Weeks later, Jane and Kennedy received an email from Detective Gabriel thanking them for their help and with the details of a replacement cruise for the following year. He had also included the verdict of Ramon and Adaline's trial. Ramon was sentenced to fifteen years for his involvement in procuring the toxin that killed Mervin. Adaline was due to be sent back to the states, where she would serve a combined sentence of fifty years without parole for the deaths of each of her husbands.

"It's funny," Jane began.

"What is?"

"Think about it; every time we go on holiday, we solve a crime. Where should we go next?"

The End

DISCOVERED ON EASTER

A COZY MYSTERY

CHAPTER 1
THE JOY OF NEW BEGINNINGS

"KENNEDY! KENNEDY! COME QUICK!" Jane screamed as she paced back and forth in the bathroom.

Kennedy ran up the stairs, her heart pounding, assuming the worst.

"What's wrong? What happened?" Kennedy panicked.

"It happened. It finally happened!" Jane croaked, tears of joy welling in her eyes.

Kennedy looked back at Jane, searching for answers before her eyes fell on the positive pregnancy test in Jane's hands.

"You're pregnant?" Kennedy gasped, her heart pounding so hard she could hear it beating in her ears.

"I'm pregnant," Jane nodded.

"We are going to have a family?" Kennedy welled up, a lump in her throat.

"It finally happened. We are going to be mums," Jane flung her arms around Kennedy.

Everything they had ever wanted was now within their grasp. It had been a long and emotional journey, but the end was near – the day when Jane and Kennedy got to hold their child in their arms.

With their history of finding trouble around the holidays, the rest of the year was spent being extra cautious. No trips abroad, no galas with the mayor. Instead, Jane and Kennedy spent the next eight months planning and decorating the nursery in neutral colours. Kennedy even grew fond of shopping with Jane. Naturally, they shopped for baby clothes, and Kennedy was determined to find the right gadgets to help the baby.

They had decided not to find out the gender; they wanted it to be a surprise. Each ultrasound picture was framed and made into a collage in the nursery; a wall dedicated to the journey of becoming parents. Jane and Kennedy marked off the calendar each day as Jane's due date approached at the start of April.

"What do you think of the name Chandler if it's a boy?" Jane asked.

"I thought we decided not to name him or her after our favourite TV show characters," Kennedy chuckled.

"Okay, then, what names do you like?" Jane asked.

Hours had passed before they had settled on one, laughing at each other's choices of names and competing over who could come up with the funniest name. The perfect name for if it was a girl or a boy. Morgan.

"Morgan, I love it," Jane smiled, hugging her enormous bump.

———

With Jane being due any day, Jane and Kennedy decided to stay close to home for Easter. In previous years, they had taken turns spending the Easter weekend with their parents; one year heading to Surrey to see Jane's family, the following heading to the States to visit Kennedy's. Not wanting to take risks, the Daniels invited their closest family and friends to their house for Easter this year.

Jane was finding it increasingly harder to walk with her large bump taking over her petite frame. So she sat at the table and spent weeks designing and decorating the perfect Easter invitations to occupy her mind. Kennedy had insisted a phone call would have sufficed, but Jane was insistent. An invitation was something the family could keep as a keepsake, not just of the night, but as a reminder of when their child was born.

"Hon, I'm sure our families will never forget the year our child was born," Kennedy teased.

"I'm fat, swollen, and practically bedridden for the next few weeks. Please let me have this one thing to stop me from going insane," Jane complained.

As the final weeks of her pregnancy approached, Jane was becoming irritable. She tried her hardest not to snap, but Kennedy found it amusing and teased Jane at every turn. Eventually, Jane realised it was Kennedy's way of showing her just how strong she was, and Jane appreciated her more for it.

"You drive me crazy.... but I love you for it," Jane winked, tossing a scrunched-up piece of paper at Kennedy after she made another joke about swollen ankles.

"I love you too, babe. Now rest those feet; I'll bring you a cup of tea."

When Kennedy returned with the tea, Jane had finally put the finishing touches on her invitations.

"How does this sound?" Jane asked, passing Kennedy the invitation.

The small square card was decorated like the cover of a murder mystery novel. It reminded Kennedy of one of her favourites, Agatha Christie's *Poirot*. The main difference was that Jane had subtly slipped baby chicks, bunnies, and easter eggs into the design. It was pretty clever and stunning. Written in the middle of the invitation in beautiful cursive gold writing read:

> To all, beware. This Easter dinner will
> not all be as it seems. Mystery will
> be the Piece de Resistance at the end
> of the Easter festivities.

"I think it's beautiful. But you know your mother will hate it. She hates surprises," Kennedy warned as she helped Jane pack the invitations into envelopes.

"She will be fine," Jane shrugged.

True enough, a few days later, when the invitations reached their recipients and the RSVPs came in, Kennedy strolled in with a smirk.

"Hi Leslie, yes, she's here; hold on,... it's your mum," Kennedy grinned, handing Jane the phone.

Jane tapped the loudspeaker button and smiled, "Hi Mum, how are you?"

"Don't give me that; what is this invitation? You know I don't like surprises. How am I supposed to enjoy dinner knowing something is going on? I will be on edge all night," Leslie complained down the phone, making Jane and Kennedy laugh.

"Oh, come on, Mum. What's the worst that can happen?"

———

"And what sort of mystery would you have us solve? What is wrong with a good old-fashioned Easter egg hunt?" Leslie groaned into the phone.

"Easter egg hunts are for kids, Mum. We are hosting a murder mystery dinner," Jane replied.

"Of course you are. You girls are something else," Leslie chuckled. "You know I'm not the only one who doesn't like surprises," she insisted.

"I know, Mum, but Rochelle and Ben haven't complained. On the contrary, they are looking forward to it."

Kennedy rolled her eyes at the mention of her parents' name and headed to her office. Rochelle and Ben were known for their competitive nature, a trait shared by Jane's mother, Leslie. Kennedy knew Jane was trying to rile up her mother to convince her the dinner would be fun.

"Oh, Rochelle and Ben are coming?" Leslie asked.

"Of course! What sort of wife would I be if I didn't invite my in-laws?"

"Oh no, it's not that.... I suppose it will make the festivities different, and it could be fun. Will there be teams? What's the set-up?" Leslie asked.

"Oh no, Mum, I'm not giving you any hints. You will have to wait for the dinner party like everyone else," Jane laughed.

Leslie was a stubborn woman and kept pushing for hints, but Jane wouldn't give up.

"You will be my death," Leslie laughed, hoping her choice of words would jolt Jane into giving something up.

"Well, we won't know that until we draw names from the hat, will we?" Jane chuckled, ending the call.

Jane waddled across the house to Kennedy's office, where Kennedy was hard at work coding a new program for a client. She worked hard for weeks, and the deadline was approaching. It was one of Kennedy's more complex orders, and Jane knew she had been struggling with it.

"How's it going?" Jane asked, placing the phone back on the receiver.

"Fine, for now anyway. The next phase will be the make-or-break; the client's requests are quite unique. I want to get it done before our dinner party and Morgan's arrival," Kennedy sighed, rubbing her hands over her face.

Jane waddled over and started massaging Kennedy's shoulders; she could feel the tension through her fingertips.

"You will be fine, honey. I believe in you," Jane kissed Kennedy's cheek.

"Thanks, babe. What can I do for my beautiful wife?"

CHAPTER 2
A SCREAM IN THE NIGHT

EASTER WAS ALWAYS a hard time for Detective Arthur Gottfried. He never told Kennedy or Jane, but ten years prior, his wife of twelve years had passed at Easter time. Arthur still blamed himself. He had been working on a tough case and drinking so he couldn't drive. Laura had been out with friends and struggled to get a ride home. Her taxi had been involved in a crash, and Arthur lost the love of his life.

"I still blame myself. If only I hadn't been drinking, I could have collected her; she would still be here," Arthur confessed to Dannie.

Arthur and Dannie had been dating for over a year, and Dannie was the first person since Laura that Arthur felt genuinely comfortable with. They had been discussing moving in together, so Arthur thought it was time to share his past with her.

"Arthur, it wasn't your fault. How do you know if you had gone to collect her, the two of you wouldn't have been involved in the crash? It's something out of your control, and I'm sure Laura wouldn't want you spending your life blaming yourself for it," Dannie comforted.

"I've never told anyone else about Laura. Jane and Kennedy don't even know about her," Arthur confessed.

"I'm truly honoured that you feel comfortable enough to share this with me," Dannie smiled.

"Why wouldn't I? I love you, Dannie," Arthur grinned.

"I love you too, Arthur," Dannie said as she kissed Arthur softly. "Speaking of Jane and Kennedy, a letter came from them today." Dannie handed Arthur the decorative envelope.

Opening it and quickly reading, Arthur burst out laughing. Then, shaking his head, he picked up his mobile and dialled Jane's number.

———

"Good morning, Arthur; how are you and Dannie?" Jane chirped.

"Wonderful, thank you. We just received your invitation. What spectacle do you have planned now?" Arthur chuckled.

"Oh, you know, a little murder mystery. Why not change things up a bit? Solving a crime around a celebration seems to be mine and Kennedy's thing. This time, I thought, why not control the fun myself?"

"Well, Dannie and I would love to come. Thank you for the invite," Arthur smiled, taking Dannie's hand.

"Wonderful," Jane cheered.

Dannie took the phone from Arthur and talked with Jane about how her pregnancy was going and about baby names. In the year since Dannie and Arthur reacquainted, Jane, Kennedy and Dannie had become quite close. The Daniels liked Dannie very much and found she brought out a happier side of Arthur; they loved seeing Arthur happy.

"I can't wait. What wine should I bring?" Dannie asked.

"You have great taste in wine; I'll let you pick."

"And I'll bring something equally as tasty and non-alcoholic for you to Jane," Arthur chirped, feeling slightly left out of the conversation.

"Wonderful, see you both soon," Jane ended the call.

———

Two days before Easter, Jane began to prepare. First, with Kennedy's help, she set up a speaker in the loft space that would alert the guests with screams of terror, letting them know festivities were about to commence when Kennedy pressed the button on her phone. Next, they scattered clues around the house and linked up speakers around the house.

"Have you figured out who the killer will be yet?" Kennedy asked.

"If I'm honest, I haven't even figured out who the victim will be," Jane admitted.

"Well, you better hurry up. The dinner is in two days."

Jane wanted every part of the property to be involved. So, clues were hidden around the kitchen, lounge, everywhere except Kennedy's office – for obvious reasons, and even the garden.

"Kennedy, can you help me with this?" Jane asked, dragging a box in from the hall.

"Jane, what are you doing? Don't be dragging anything heavy. What is it?"

"It's a scarecrow I ordered to play the victim's body. I know our mothers wouldn't be happy if they pulled out the victim's name and had to sit the rest of the game out, so...."

Kennedy ripped open the box and immediately jumped back. The scarecrow had come from a website dedicated to murder mysteries, and the prop didn't disappoint. The scarecrow was dressed in a dinner suit with fake blood drenching its once crisp white shirt. The face looked almost human, with soft to the touch skin – An expression of horror and wide eyes depict the look of lifeless eyes.

"Jane, that's terrifying," Kennedy gasped, clutching her hand to her chest.

"I know it's great, isn't it? And it was cheap, a discontinued line."

"I can see why," Kennedy laughed, scooping up the fake body and flinging it over her shoulder.

"So, where is he going?" Kennedy asked.

"The garden shed, between the wheelbarrow and the potted plans."

"I just hope none of the neighbours are looking out their window; otherwise, they will like we have killed someone if they see me trudging this thing across the lawn," Kennedy laughed.

On the morning of the Easter dinner, Jane began her day by preparing the vegetables she would cook later. With the vegetables prepped, she started blending her secret basting mixture; even Kennedy didn't know the list of ingredients. Then, scoring the lamb, Jane rubbed her secret recipe into the meat before popping it into the oven to slow roast for the rest of the day. Jane's lamb was famous throughout the family. It was always so tender and juicy that it fell clean off the bone.

"I definitely smell garlic and rosemary," Kennedy said, popping her head into the kitchen.

"I'm still not telling you my secret recipe," Jane teased, washing her hands.

"You are going to have to tell me one day."

Jane shook her head and playfully stuck out her tongue, making Kennedy laugh.

"Jane, there is something I have been wanting to ask you for a while now, but I'm worried about the answer," Kennedy said, keeping her eyes cast down.

"What's wrong, honey? You know you can ask me anything," Jane said, waddling over to Jane and taking her hands in hers.

"It's nothing too big, just a concern of mine."

Jane was beginning to panic; she and Kennedy had never had issues communicating. What could have Kennedy so concerned?

"Baby, talk to me," Jane worried.

"It's just about dinner, the murder mystery thing......please tell me you haven't got us costumes," Kennedy mocked, her act breaking as she began to laugh.

"Oh, Kennedy, you are so mean. I was so worried for a second. And to answer your question, no, I haven't, but I wouldn't say no to getting dolled up. It's still a family occasion, after all."

"Of course," Kennedy kissed Jane before heading upstairs.

Jane had thought about making the event a fancy-dress party, getting into the whole spirit of a good murder mystery. But when she couldn't find a suitable costume for herself, given her huge baby bump, she decided against it. She didn't want to be the only one not dressed for the occasion.

Instead, she opted for a simple black floor-length dress, flat sandals, and accessories with gold jewellery. Kennedy had opted for a teal suit with a white shirt; she looked beautiful.

The guest list consisted of Jane's parents, Kennedy's parents, Arthur and Dannie, Jane's cousin Lucia and a few other relatives and friends from college. Jane couldn't wait to see everyone again; she hadn't seen Lucia before she was arrested on Boxing Day. It had been even longer since Kennedy had seen her parents other than via a computer screen. Jane and Kennedy had been so busy travelling to Italy to return the stolen jewels, Kennedy's near miss on Halloween and then Jane breaking her leg. Then, with Valentine's Day the year before marking their first steps to getting pregnant and Jane studying for her private investigator licence, life had got in the way of family visits. With a new addition to the family only days away, it was the perfect time for a family get-together.

CHAPTER 3
SUSPICIONS AND SECRETS

A ROW of cars lined the street outside Jane and Kennedy's home –
Cars of all shapes, sizes, and vintages. Classic cars were a long-lost
hobby of Arthur. So, when his eyes fell on a cherry red 1957 Jaguar
Roadster, it took all he had not to geek out. He wondered whom the
car might belong to. Eyeing all the cars was a welcome distraction
from the nerves bubbling in his stomach. But he didn't have time to
study the cars. They had a dinner date to attend.

"Arthur, are you okay?" Dannie asked as Arthur stood outside the
door, hesitant to ring the doorbell.

"I'm just a little nervous. I don't really know anyone except Jane
and Kennedy. I wonder what their families are like; I heard stories,
but...."

"You are not alone. I'm here with you. Come on, ring the bell,"
Dannie urged softly.

Arthur stood a little taller, nodding and smiling back at the woman
he loved before pressing the bell. As Dannie and Arthur stood waiting,
it was evident that the line of cars belonged to the many voices inside
the house. Roars of laughter and chatter could be heard even through
the thick wooden door.

"Arthur, Dannie, it's so good to see you. Sorry it took so long to answer. As you can see, it's getting harder and harder to move around," Jane laughed, rubbing her round belly.

"Wow, Jane, you look ready to pop," Dannie joked, making Arthur's face erupt in horror, only to make the women laugh harder.

"Any day now," Jane ushered the pair inside.

The house was full of people gathered, chatting and laughing. Some Arthur recognised from pictures around the Daniels' home. Kennedy joined her wife in greeting Arthur and Dannie before taking them around the house and introducing everyone.

"Arthur, this is my mother, Leslie and my father, George," Jane introduced. "Mum, Dad, this is Detective Arthur Gottfried and his girl-friend, Doctor Danielle Fitzpatrick."

"Please, call me Dannie," Dannie smiled, shaking Leslie and George's hands.

"Pleasure to meet you both. We have heard great things about you, Detective Gottfried. You have quite the fan club with my daughter and daughter-in-law," George boasted.

"That's so kind, but I am a fan of theirs. They are wonderful people," Arthur smiled back, blushing slightly.

Arthur had never been one to accept or give compliments easily. Dannie gently squeezed his hand, letting him know everything was okay. She had positively influenced him, opening him up to new things and letting his softer, gentler side come to the surface.

"The first course is almost ready if everyone would like to take their seats," Jane chirped, leading everyone into the dining room.

————

The dining room was decorated in shades of white, dusky pink, and brown to match the clues and decorations scattered across the table. The long dining table was big enough to fit sixteen guests, covered in a white lace tablecloth with a dusky pink chiffon runner down the centre. Candles of all shapes and sizes were scattered in the middle of the table, mixed with mystery-themed props. Magnifying glasses, white cotton gloves, a monocle, and a tobacco pipe were just a few decorations sitting pride of place. Still, as it was an Easter celebration,

Jane had also included small mini easter eggs, figurine bunnies, and chicks scattered throughout the room. On each place setting was a napkin wrapped in red ribbon with an envelope with the word *clue* written in gold ink.

Each place setting had each person's name. To throw everyone off the scent and get everyone to know each other a little better, Jane had purposely split couples up and mixed the families in the seating arrangements.

"What? I'm not sitting with your father?" Leslie groaned.

"Come, Mrs Devon, it shall be fun," Arthur chimed, pulling out Leslie's chair for her as his name was next to hers.

"Don't worry, Leslie, I'll keep an eye on George for you," Dannie teased, winking at Arthur taking her seat next to George.

"Where are we sitting?" asked Rochelle, Kennedy's mother.

"Next to me," came Lucia's voice.

It took a while for all the guests to find their assigned seats. Jane and Kennedy allowed everyone to finish their drinks and aquatint themselves before filling their glasses and serving the first course, which Rochelle had graciously provided. Bistro salad with goat's cheese croutes. Everyone had come prepared with some dish to help take some pressure off Jane, leaving her to spend her time on the main course and the mystery games for the evening.

"Wow, Rochelle. This salad is delicious," Leslie chimed.

"Thank you, it's so simple, really. It's a goat's cheese base with fresh lettuce, my special secret mixture of herbs and a homemade mustard vinaigrette. I fell in love with the recipe when I studied in Paris," Rochelle explained.

"It will pair nicely with the wine Yvette brought," chimed Jane's cousin Amanda as she handed Kennedy the bottle of Sauvignon Blanc.

"So, when does the mystery start?" George asked, eager to get involved.

George was probably the most competitive member of the group. He had been itching to open his clue since he sat down, but Leslie had given him a glare telling him to wait until everyone else opened theirs.

"While I clear up the first course, everyone, feel free to read your clues. But remember, don't share the details with the other players," Jane winked.

———

"Oh, how exciting. I will admit, I wasn't too enthused about a murder mystery dinner. But Jane, you have done such a wonderful job, and this clue intrigued me," chimed Kennedy's old college tutor, Mrs Tree.

Mrs Tree had always been known for being outspoken. She cared little for what people thought of her and always encouraged her students to speak their minds freely. "Nothing ventured, nothing gained. Regrets form by unspoken words and plans not put into action," was her catchphrase.

"Shush, Andrea, don't give anything away," nudged her husband, Ronald.

"Oh, don't be silly, Ronald, as if I would ever let a thing slip," Mrs Tree waved dismissively.

As the quests chatted amongst themselves, Jane and Kennedy beamed with pride. This was precisely what they had hoped for. The perfect blend of their family, enjoying each other's company before Morgan made an appearance. Seeing the mix of people, personalities, and viewpoints that would influence their child warmed the heart. Wisdom from generations; it took a village to raise a child, and the Daniels were ecstatic with the village of people they had in their corner.

Jane grabbed Kennedy's hand, placing it on her stomach as little Morgan kicked away.

"Morgan can feel the love from everyone too," Jane whispered.

"He or she can't wait to meet her family. He or she knows how much love awaits," Kennedy kissed Jane's head softly.

Jane had prepared two cocktail menus as some of Jane's cousins were under eighteen. One for the adults and one that she and the younger guests could enjoy.

"Oooh, can I have the basil and lime lemonade?" asked Lucia.

"Sure, I'll join you. Any other cocktail requests?" Jane asked the room.

"What's the easter bunny cocktail?" asked Kennedy.

Jane had changed her mind about the drink menu so many times over the previous days that some of the cocktails were a surprise to her too.

"Oh, it's beautiful. I found the recipe online. It's got a kick to it, so don't drink too many. It's vodka, chocolate liquor, cherry brandy, and chocolate-flavoured sugar syrup. But I also add a splash of blackcurrant liquor," Jane beamed with pride at her creation.

"You are trying to get us all drunk, aren't you?" laughed Ben raising his glass of whiskey.

"Well, if I can't drink, I just want to make sure everyone else has fun on my behalf," Jane joked.

————

With her father's help, Jane brought the lamb to serve at the table. George insisted his daughter sit down and allow him to carve while Kennedy brought out the honey-roasted Gammon and began to carve. A delectable combination of smells filled the room; mouths watered as everyone passed around the serving plates, selecting their chosen vegetables. Jane had thought of everything. The main course consisted of Jane's famous glazed slow-cooked lamb, honey-roasted Gammon and slow-roasted beef. There was a selection for everyone. She had also prepared salmon for her cousins, who had recently shifted to a pescatarian diet and vegetarian options of aubergine, courgette, and asparagus for some of the other guests, along with mashed, boiled, and roasted potatoes. The guests were spoilt for choice. Jane had also prepared Yorkshire puddings, a mix of herb-roasted vegetables, stuffing, and gravies.

"Wow, Jane, you really have spoilt us. This food is delicious," Dannie smiled.

"Well, I wanted today to be special," Jane beamed.

As the guests tucked into their food, Jane grew even more emotional. Flooded with joy, love, and gratitude, she couldn't keep it to herself any longer. Pushing her chair back, she stood with tears in her eyes, tapping a spoon to her glass to draw everyone's attention.

"Sorry to interrupt your meal, but I have a few things I want to say," Jane began.

Reaching for Kennedy's hand, she looked at her wife with a heart filled to bursting.

"Kennedy, you have given me more than you will ever know. You have brought joy to my life and made me a better version of myself. Words cannot express how happy I am that we are about to start the next phase of our lives together.....Arthur, it is with your help and influence that I felt the confidence to chase my dream, and for that, I can never thank you enough....Dannie, you make Arthur happier than I have ever seen, you are a truly amazing person, and I am honoured to call you my friend...."

Jane went round the room in turn, showering her guests with love and admiration. As she looked at the smiling faces of her family and friends, Jane noticed she wasn't the only one overcome, eyes glistened like stars with tears of joy. The room buzzed with warmth and electricity that only family can bring.

"I'm sorry, call it pregnancy hormones, but what I'm trying to say is, I love you all so much. I am so grateful that our little one will have such an amazing group of people to help guide and influence him or her. Wow, I guess dreams do come true because I am filled with so much gratitude right now. Everything I have ever wanted and everyone I have ever loved is right here in these walls," Jane smiled, wiping a stray tear from her eye.

Kennedy stood with her wife, hugging her tightly as her guests clapped and cheered, sharing in an embrace.

"Shall we tell them?" Kennedy whispered.

Jane nodded and took Kennedy's hand while holding her bump with the other.

"Ladies and gentlemen, we have an announcement to make," Kennedy said.

"Oh my god, you're pregnant," Lucia joked, making the group howl with laughter.

"We have hinted but are finally ready to reveal our chosen name. Be it a boy or a girl, we would like you all to welcome.... Morgan," Kennedy cheered.

———

With the main course finished, George and Ben helped clear the table. With everyone fully relaxed, Jane and Kennedy agreed it was time to get the mystery underway. Kennedy slipped her hand under the table and pressed the button on her phone. A bloodcurdling, bone-chilling scream erupted through the house, playing through the many scattered speakers Kennedy had programmed. Mrs Tree jumped, dropping her champagne flute and shattering it on the floor.

"A bit extreme, don't you think, honey?" Jane asked, raising an eyebrow at Kennedy.

"I didn't listen to the track before I loaded it. I found it online," Kennedy shrugged.

Ronald and Mrs Tree hurried to clean up their mess as the guests slowly realised the games had begun. They were eyeing each other with suspicion. Some rechecked their clues before the room erupted in question.

"What was that?"

"Has the game begun?"

"Who screamed?"

"Where did it come from?"

Jane and Kennedy chuckled, watching as their loved ones' competitive sides kicked in and people teamed up to hunt for clues around the house. Following the screams, everyone was reluctant to go into the loft space.

"Well done, ladies. This is going to be fun," Arthur grinned, teaming up with Kennedy's uncle Lucas, a fellow police officer.

Jane sat back, watching her mother scratching her head, trying to figure out the riddle she had found hidden in the pictures on the mantle. Leslie kept a close eye on Rochelle, determined to beat her, as did Rochelle with Leslie. It was proving a great form of entertainment.

"Okay, so our first mystery is deciphering who was killed and where?" Dannie asked.

"Exactly; if all the guests were in the dining room, who could the victim be?" Lucia asked.

"I honestly thought the victim would be one of us," Yvette said.

"Why would I do that? Then one of you would have to sit the game out because you would be dead. This way, everyone can get involved," Jane smiled.

As the guests dispersed around the home, suddenly Rochelle came charging down the stairs waving a clue in hand, excited she had figured out the next step.

"I found this in the attack," she cheered.

"What does it say?" Leslie asked.

Rochelle unfolded the piece of paper and read the clue aloud to all the guests.

"You have looked high; now it's time to look low. Before you know it, my name you will know."

CHAPTER 4
A CLUE IN THE SHED

"YOU GUYS DON'T HAVE a basement, do you?" Ben asked.

"No, Dad. Basements aren't really a feature in UK homes," Kennedy laughed.

As the guests tried to decipher their clues, putting together puzzles and answering riddles, leading them to the next clue, another scream erupted. Unfortunately, while this scream didn't echo through each room in the house, it was just as terrifying.

"What, another victim?" Lucia asked, frustrated as she had just worked out her latest clue.

"No, Kennedy must have pressed the button by mistake," Jane answered.

"No, I didn't. My phone is on charge in the office," Kennedy said, confused, looking to Jane for answers.

Panicked, Jane waddled from room to room, checking that all her loved ones were safe and unharmed, while Kennedy rushed upstairs to check on the budding detectives upstairs. Everyone was present and accounted for, and everyone had heard the scream.

Unsure what was happening, the guests gathered in the dining room, looking at each other to see who had screamed. Was it an effort to throw the others off their game? Was someone closer to winning than Jane and Kennedy would have liked so early on in the game?

"It sounded like it came from outside," Dannie said.

"No one has been in the garden," Jane said.

That fact annoyed Jane; she thought she had made her clues simple enough for even a novice detective to gather that the clues were leading them to the garden shed.

"It might just be next door, kids. They probably heard the scream and wanted to be involved in the game, too," Leslie shrugged.

Kennedy and Arthur's eyes locked; something wasn't quite right.

"Tell you what, let me go have a look outside," Arthur nodded, heading into the garden alone.

———

The house grew thick with tension as everyone waited for Arthur to return. Dannie waited anxiously at the window, fiddling with the star and moon pendant hanging around her neck. Leslie and Rochelle were still in game mode, working through their clues and sneaking a peak at others.

"How about we tuck into the dessert while we wait to continue the game? We have plenty to choose from," Jane smiled, heading to the kitchen.

Jane had prepared her famous carrot cake and decorated it with vanilla buttercream. Leslie had brought chocolate brownies and Rochelle, her famous pecan pie. Arthur had brought a Victoria sponge – shop-bought, as he burnt his first and second attempt at baking. Everyone seemed to bring a dessert. As Kennedy and Jane lay the desserts on the table, they realised they had too much. Cakes, pies, cupcakes, cookies, they would have dessert for days.

"I'll make a pot of tea and coffee, too," Kennedy whispered, keeping a close eye on the shed.

Everyone could see Arthur pacing back and forth from the dining room windows in front of the shed. He had his phone in hand, in deep conversation. Dannie tugged harder on her necklace, feeling Arthur's tension even from a distance.

Jane and Kennedy busied themselves, trying to defuse the tension. Finally, Jane convinced Lucia to perform her latest drama monologue from college to entertain the guests. Initially, she was reluctant, but her performance was so captivating that it proved just what the group needed.

———

Arthur snuck back in, careful not to alarm anyone. He pulled Kennedy and Dannie to one side. His face was troubled, and his brow furrowed.

"We need to keep everyone inside. This is now an active crime scene," Arthur whispered.

"What? The dummy in the shed is fake, Arthur. I know how realistic it looked; I jumped myself when I opened the box," Kennedy chuckled, not believing their home could be the scene of a crime.

"The dummy isn't the only body in there," Arthur said.

"Oh, my goodness," Dannie gasped.

"I've called the forensic team and the ME, but until they get here, Dannie, would you mind taking a look and see what you think the cause of death could be?" Arthur asked.

"Of course," Dannie agreed, following Arthur back outside.

Kennedy looked at the party guests as they clapped and cheered at Lucia's performance. Jane was so happy. Kennedy's heart sank that she would have to ruin Jane's evening. Kennedy also worried about what the undue stress would do to Jane and the baby. Sighing, deciding it was better to pull the plaster off in one go, she tapped Jane on the shoulder, pulling her into the kitchen away from the group.

"Don't panic, but someone is dead in the shed," Kennedy blurted out.

"What?" Jane gasped.

"That scream was someone being murdered. Dannie and Arthur are examining the body now, and the ME and a forensic team are on the way. The police will be swarming the house in no time," Kennedy warned.

"What are we going to do? Who is it?" Jane asked, rubbing her baby bump in concern.

"I don't know."

———

"Do you know this man?" Arthur asked, showing the Daniels a picture of the body in their shed.

"Oh my gosh, that's Mr Wolf from next door," Jane gasped.

"What was he doing in our shed?" Kennedy wondered.

"We can figure that out when the forensic team arrives. But, right now, we need to find out where everyone was at the time of the murder," Arthur ran his hands through his thick greying hair.

Nodding with sombre faces, Jane and Kennedy headed back to their guests. Slowly they explained the situation as best they could.

"Jeez, Jane. When you said murder mystery dinner, I didn't think you would commit so strongly to the performance," Lucia joked.

"This is no joke, I'm afraid. The police will be here any minute," Jane sighed.

The room fell silent. No one believed a word, all waiting and hoping someone would jump up and say it was all part of the game. How could it not be?

"Wait, you're serious?" Ben asked.

Kennedy nodded, and the room fell into an uncomfortable silence.

"So, we are all suspects then, right?" Yvette asked.

Again, Kennedy nodded, and the room took on a new type of tension. Looks of sorrow turned to looks of concern before eventually turning to looks of suspicion. A once harmonious, loving group now all eyed each other in fear. Jane felt her chest grow tight, and she stroked her hand softly over her heart to try and ease her tension.

"Oooh," Jane gasped lightly, clutching her hand to her side.

Baby Morgan was feeling the tension too.

It's Braxton-hicks, that's all. Morgan isn't due for another week; Jane convinced herself.

CHAPTER 5
THE STEPDAUGHTER'S ALIBI

ONCE THE POLICE and forensic teams arrived, everyone split into separate rooms. Rochelle and Ben headed to the spare room, Leslie and George headed to Jane and Kennedy's room, and the other guests divided between the kitchen, lounge, dining room, and living room. Jane sat on the sofa, rubbing the right side of her belly. The stress of having her loved ones questioned brought on pains that she kept trying to ignore.

When Mrs Tree noticed the neighbours gathering outside their homes looking for gossip on what had happened inside, she took it upon herself to close all the curtains to offer privacy. Yet all it did was cast darkness, matching the atmosphere that unnerved everyone further.

Kennedy bounced between Arthur and the officers and ensured the guests were topped up with tea and coffee. Seconds felt like minutes, minutes felt like hours, as the police questioned each guest in turn, not wanting to let anyone go until they had more answers.

"Jane, you need to rest," Kennedy worried as Jane joined her at the kitchen window.

"I'm going crazy sitting and doing nothing. I need to know what's going on," Jane sighed, rubbing her belly a little more.

"So far, I've been told nothing. Even Arthur has been pushed out as he is technically a suspect too."

"He won't be happy with that," Jane said.

Arthur's partner, Lieutenant Harper, had taken over the investigation. Arthur tried his hardest to get involved but was warned that he would be arrested for obstruction if he didn't stay out of it. Arthur paced the hallway anxiously as Dannie sat on the stairs, watching, playing with her necklace.

———

By the time the forensic team left, it was early morning hours, and Mr Wolf's body was taken from the scene. Arthur, Jane, Kennedy, and Dannie headed into the garden to speak with Lieutenant Harper.

"Do you know what happened?" Dannie asked when the others were all too nervous to speak.

"It looks like he was stabbed several times. Whomever it was, was angry because these puncture marks are too deep and frantic to be self-defence. But I can also rule out anyone inside as a suspect," Lieutenant Harper said.

"How so?" Arthur asked.

"Skins cells under the deceased fingernails says he fought back. None of your guests had scratches on them. Also, there is a void in the blood on the floor where the killer stands. Finally, none of your guests has blood on their shoes," Harper answered.

"So you are saying Mr Wolf was killed inside the shed? He wasn't dragged there? Who would come into someone else's garden just to kill someone?" Jane panicked.

"I'd say someone who wanted to frame you two for the murder," Dannie said sadly.

"We are just gathering the last bits of evidence, then we will be out of your hair," Harper patted Kennedy on the shoulder.

A team of forensic officers emerged from the shed carrying items splattered with blood, including Jane's life-like dummy from the party.

"Wait, something is missing," Jane yelled, waddling over to the officer holding the dummy.

"Please don't touch, miss."

"Kennedy look, the knife is missing," Jane pointed to the hole in the dummy's chest.

"Knife?" Arthur asked.

"Yeah, the dummy had a knife plunged in its chest. It came like that from the prop store. I never thought it was a real knife. If anything, I thought the hilt was glued on," Jane gasped.

"You don't think that's the murder weapon, do you?" Kennedy asked.

"I'm sure we find the killer when we find the knife. We start interviewing your neighbours tomorrow," Harper said, urging the officers to leave.

———

With Lieutenant Harper giving the guests the all-clear to leave, Jane and Kennedy bid everyone a good night. Everyone was ordered to hand their passports to the station the following morning. No one was to leave town until the killer had been caught.

"Jane, I'm worried about you. You have been rubbing your stomach all day. Is everything okay? Should we go to the hospital?" Kennedy asked as she helped Jane to bed.

"No, I'm fine. It's Braxton-hicks, you know, false labour. It's probably due to the stress. So don't worry," Jane smiled, but her eyes held concern.

Kennedy knew not to push and decided to stay up all night to tend to Jane. Jane didn't sleep much either that night. The few times Kennedy's eyes had grown too heavy, Jane had slipped out of bed and downstairs. Kennedy found her at the kitchen window, staring out at the shed.

"Baby, come back to bed," Kennedy yawned.

"Why would someone want to frame us?" Jane asked, a lump in her throat.

"Lieutenant Harper will figure that out, sweetie. All you need to worry about now is little Morgan," Kennedy yawned, gently urging Jane back to bed.

No matter what Jane tried, that night's sleep wouldn't come. All she could see whenever she closed her eyes was her long-time neighbour dead in her shed. She had known Mr Wolf for years, and he had always been a pillar of the community. He was the type of man to go out of his way to help, always had a smile and was loved by everyone. Jane wracked her mind to think of a reason someone would want to kill him in such an angry and violent way.

———

By dinner time the following day, Kennedy had tried everything to get Jane to eat, but she had no appetite. Then, still suffering from Braxton-hicks, Jane thought that Kennedy had the right idea. If the pain didn't stop, she would agree to go to the hospital.

A knock on the door offered the distraction Jane needed, and Arthur had returned alone. After being cleared as a suspect, Lieutenant Harper had agreed to allow him to help with the investigation. Arthur had spent all day interviewing the neighbours and had already devised a theory of his own.

"So you think his wife killed him and then took off?" Kennedy asked, handing Arthur a leftover piece of carrot cake.

"That's what it looks like. Mr Wolf's stepdaughter Denise seemed pretty upset. She said her mother and stepfather had been arguing. Denise had gone to her room and put on her headphones stuck in a video game to mask the sounds of yelling. She said she hadn't seen her mother since," Arthur said between bites.

"You don't think that's the entire story, do you?" Jane asked.

Arthur shook his head, taking another bite of cake and a sip of tea. Dabbing his mouth, Jane could practically see the cog turning in his mind as he tried to piece together the mystery.

"We tracked Mrs Wolf's car via CCTV. She was at her mother's house twenty-five miles away at the time of the murder. I think the stepdaughter had something to do with it. She kept pulling at her sleeves, ensuring her arms were covered, and from the witness reports, the scream they heard was female," Arthur stated.

"But what would her motive be?" Kennedy asked.

"That's what we need to figure out."

CHAPTER 6
THE MURDER WEAPON REVEALED

THE NEXT DAY at the police station, Lieutenant Harper and Detective Gottfried gathered what evidence they had so far and pinned it to the bulletin board. The centre was a picture of Mr Wolf's body from the shed. Next was a line of suspects – his wife and stepdaughter. They wrote the time of death, the murder weapon and a few other details and stepped back to review it.

"What's that?" Arthur asked, pointing to the CCTV footage of Mrs Wolf's car.

"That's his wife," Harper replied.

Arthur took a step closer, examining the grainy image of a woman wearing sunglasses and a hat. The woman looked much younger than Arthur had thought she would be to have a sixteen-year-old daughter.

"That's not Mrs Wolf," Arthur said, pulling the image down and looking closer.

"It's her car."

"But that's not her driving," Arthur pointed out.

"What's this?" Arthur asked, pointing to another image of Mr Wolf's body.

"It's the crime scene. Arthur, are you feeling, okay?"

"I told you I should have been involved from the get-go," Arthur shook his head.

In the few hours they had been reviewing what Harper had gathered so far, Arthur was already noticing details that should have been glaringly obvious. Shaking his head, Arthur took the image and headed out of the room.

"Where are you going?" Harper yelled after him.

"To the evidence locker and to get a warrant," Arthur replied.

———

Arthur had done the right thing. His main suspect was about to board a plane to Europe when his team apprehended her. The killer might have gotten away if Arthur had figured it out just a few minutes later.

The evidence was shaky at best, but Arthur knew that once he got a confession, the evidence wouldn't matter. And Arthur knew he had enough evidence to make the suspect shake in her boots.

Staring through the double-sided glass, Arthur watched as Denise paced the room, still pulling her sleeves past her hands. Arthur waited a little longer until she sat down, rocking her chair back and forward before sitting straight and bouncing her leg anxiously.

"Harper, come on, we have work to do," Arthur grunted, leading the way to interrogation room C.

Photographs, a warrant, a gold button, and a name were all Arthur had to go on. They still didn't have the murder weapon, but Arthur knew he had the right person in custody.

———

"Hello, Miss Wolf," Arthur said, taking a seat.

"My name isn't Wolf. I have my biological father's last name," Denise said, keeping her eyes on her hands.

"Oh, I know," Arthur grinned, watching as Denise's entire demeanour changed.

"You can't interview me alone. I'm a minor. I need a parent or guardian or a lawyer with me," Denise said, suddenly confident.

"Your father is on his way," Arthur said, sitting back and folding his arms.

Arthur began to mirror Denise, leaning back in his chair and rocking it on the back legs. Then, keeping his eyes trained on her, he waited silently.

The clock's ticking and the chairs' creak were the only sounds. The clock sounded louder with every passing second. Even to Arthur, it was maddening, but it seemed to be doing the trick in agitating Denise more.

A knock on the door alerted the detectives to Martin Cox's arrival. Now things could truly begin.

———

"Thank you for coming, Mr Cox," Lieutenant Harper said, shaking the man's hand.

"Of course, my sweet girl is accused of murder. Where else would I be? Now can we get this nonsense over with? I want to take my daughter home," Martin groaned, sitting close to his daughter.

"Right then. Denise, when did your mother leave?" Arthur asked.

"I don't know. I was playing my video games."

"For an entire eight weeks? Because her passport was logged heading to America eight weeks ago. Last known location was Ohio," Arthur said, pulling the record from the folder in his lap and sliding it across the table.

"Don't say anything, honey," Martin whispered, glaring at Arthur.

"Is this you?" Arthur asked, sliding the picture of Denise driving her mother's car.

"I don't have my licence yet."

"That's not what I asked," Arthur smirked.

"If this is all you have, I'm taking my daughter home now, and I'm putting in a complaint with the police chief," Martin said, standing and grabbing his daughter's arm.

"Sit down, Mr Cox; I will get to you in a second," Arthur snapped, glaring back at Martin until he sat down.

CHAPTER 7
NEW LIFE, NEW MYSTERIES

DAYS HAD PASSED since Mr wolf's murder, and it was time to explain precisely what had happened to the Daniels. As Arthur and Dannie pulled up to Jane and Kennedy's house, the same line of cars sat outside, including the cherry red Jaguar Arthur hadn't been able to stop thinking about.

Knocking on the door, Kennedy answered with a smile, immediately wrapping Dannie and Arthur in a big hug.

"It's so good to see you come in; there is someone I want you to meet," Kennedy led them through to the living room.

Sitting on the sofa, wrapped in a little blue blanket in Leslie's arms, was a beautiful baby boy. Thick dark ringlets of hair sprouted on his head, and large brown eyes blinked at the sea of smiling faces admiring him before he gently slipped back to sleep.

"Arthur, Dannie, meet Morgan," Jane smiled.

Jane was still very tired and was happy to let her relatives enjoy cuddling Morgan or two as the tiny bundle of joy was passed from relative to relative.

"Congratulations. When did you go into labour?" Dannie asked, leaning in to hug Jane.

"The night of the murder. I had been having what I thought was

Braxton-hicks all day. At half four in the morning, my waters finally broke. Kennedy delivered Morgan at home."

"You did?" Arthur gasped.

"Yeah, I called the ambulance, but Jane's labour progressed really quickly. So with the help of the nine-nine-nine operator, I delivered Morgan," Kennedy beamed with pride, joining Jane on the sofa and wrapping an arm around her shoulder.

"Wait, if Dannie and Arthur didn't know that you had given birth, they didn't come round to see the baby. Why are they here?" Lucia asked.

"Lucia, don't be rude," Leslie snapped.

"It's fine. You are quite the detective, Lucia. In fact, it's a good thing everyone is here. We have solved Mr Wolf's murder," Arthur said.

———

Getting everyone a cup of tea and a slice of cake and finding Dannie and Arthur a chair, George and the others sat waiting anxiously for every detail of the case.

"It was his wife, wasn't it?" shot one voice.

"Why was he killed in the shed?"

"Who killed him?" came another voice.

"What was the motive?"

Settling everyone down, Arthur sipped his tea, waiting for the room to quiet.

"One question at a time, please," Arthur grinned, secretly loving all eyes on him.

"How did you figure it out?" Kennedy asked, taking hold of her son.

Arthur proceeded to explain how when he had interviewed the neighbours, Denise's demeanour had piqued his interest. She insisted on keeping her arms covered, and her jacket was missing a button. When Arthur was allowed to join the case, he noticed a gold button in the crime scene photos, covered in Mr Wolf's blood. When he saw that the CCTV of Mrs Wolf showed a much younger woman, he completed a search for her passport and credit cards and found she had left for

America eight weeks before. He continued to say that he had checked Denise's gaming ID and found she hadn't logged on for three days before the murder, a detail that blew apart her alibi.

"Wait, Denise killed him? But she is a child," Jane gasped.

"She didn't do it alone," Dannie said.

"Then who did?" Rochelle asked eagerly for another hold of Morgan.

"Her father. Martin Cox."

———

"Why?" George asked.

George explained how Mrs Wolf had left weeks prior and as Denise and Mr Wolf had already had a shaky relationship, he never supported her 'gaming career', calling it a pipe dream and a non-starter. However, a week before his murder, Denise was scheduled to travel to Southampton for a gaming competition where the grand prize was a contract with Supersonic Gaming and one hundred thousand pounds.

"When I finally presented her with all the evidence I had, which at this point was very little and circumstantial at best, she cracked. She broke into tears and said that Mr Wolf had torn up her tickets and taken away her games console...."

"Wow, you rest a lot on a bluff, Arthur," Kennedy said.

"Thankfully, it worked," Arthur replied.

"So, she killed him over a game console?" Ben gasped in disgust.

"Not just the console. I looked into her supposed career. For a sixteen-year-old kid, she was pulling in six figures a year. It was just a game to her stepfather, but she had made a lot of money streaming and creating manuals for amateur gamers. After that, she got in touch with her father, asking if she could go live with him, but Mr wolf refused," Arthur stopped to take a sip of tea.

"So, she killed him because of that? What did her father have to do with it? Is he the one who put the body in the shed?" Lucia asked, hooked on the story like it was a soap opera.

"Turns out her rival won the competition she was due to enter. A gamer of much less skill than her," Dannie said, taking hold of Morgan and swaddling him close.

"So, if she had entered, chances are she would have won the contract and the prize money," Jane said.

"Exactly," Arthur nodded.

———

Arthur continued to tell the group how Denise had cracked in interrogation, screaming with rage until her father jumped in to protect her.

"I saw the two women from next door put a Halloween prop in the shed, so I thought if I could get Andrew in there, it would look like they killed him, not me," Denise had cried.

"He took me away from my dad and drove my mother away, then tried to destroy my career. Do you know what my life would be like if I had won that contract? And I would have won, you know!" Denise screamed.

"I told him I needed help with the lawn mower they said I could borrow, and when he entered the shed with me, I grabbed the shovel and hit him with it. When he went down, I called my dad to come and get me." Denise had sobbed.

Arthur sat back, arms folded, letting the two incriminate each other, making his job that much easier.

"When I arrived, I heard her scream and ran into the garden next door. Her hand was bleeding. That creep had attacked her, and she had fought back. So, it was self-defence," Martin insisted.

"It's funny you should say that because I have a warrant here to examine Denise's arms and to take a sample of her skin cells," Lieutenant Harper chimed in, tossing the warrant from his pocket on the table.

"I think Denise is telling the truth, but I also think that before you arrived, Mr Cox that Mr Wolf woke up and fought back. I think it began as self-defence on his part, and Denise stabbed him. Then, when you arrived, you saw the man trying to keep your daughter away from you and stabbed him five more times," Arthur said.

"I want my lawyer," Martin Cox demanded.

———

"I told you that stupid dummy was excessive," Kennedy mocked.

"Noted. No more murder mystery dinners," Jane laughed.

"What else? What else?" Lucia cheered, earning a round of shushes from the group as she almost woke Morgan.

"I was right, of course. When Mr Wolf woke up, he tried to escape, but Denise had pulled the knife. He scratched her arm, and when she stabbed him, she sliced her hand. When Mr Cox arrived, he finished the job, leaving Mr Wolf in the shed. When we came out to investigate, they hurried back around the bushes into their garden, and Denise dressed as he mother and took her car. A few miles between her and her grandmother's house, Denise disposed of the murder weapon. We retrieved it this morning. It's quite clever, really. She thought if she was seen on CCTV dressed as her mother and the murder weapon was found, it would implicate Mrs Wolf for the murder," Arthur continued.

"Why frame her mother?" Dannie asked.

"She was hurt that her mother had ripped her from her father and abandoned her when her marriage fell apart. She is a furious kid who needs help."

———

As the weeks passed since Mr Wolf's murder, news of the famous gamer who killed her stepfather spread like wildfire. But, with both Denise and Martin confessing, the trial was short. Martin was sentenced to twenty years for first-degree murder. And since Denise was still a minor, she could only be sentenced to two years in juvenile detention before becoming an adult and being released.

"That doesn't seem fair. She practically got away with it," Jane complained.

"Unfortunately, that's the way the law works. We can't re-try her as an adult once she turns eighteen. Juvenile detention can only hold her until she is legally an adult," Arthur sighed.

Even with a killer behind bars, the victory was bittersweet. Justice didn't feel like it had been done.

"Please tell me she isn't moving back here when she gets out?" Jane panicked, clutching baby Morgan closer to her.

"No, Mr Wolf's oldest son is selling the house. I don't know what will happen to Denise when she gets out. Unless his mother returns from the States, she has no one else. Her father was her only relative."

"What about her grandmother?" Kennedy asked.

"She wants nothing to do with her," Dannie finished.

"It's heartbreaking. A man is dead, and a kid's life is ruined because of a moment's anger. My heart goes out to Mr Wolf's son. How awful must it feel knowing your father's killer will be set free in two years?" Jane sighed.

"Technically, Mr Cox killed him. He was still alive when he arrived. So the most Denise could be charged with was ABH."

––––––––

As the weeks passed and all the drama surrounding Mr Wolf's murder subsided, Jane and Kennedy settled into family life. Jane would find herself watching her son sleep for hours, just watching him breathe.

Kennedy had rigged the nursery with all the latest tech. She had set up a starlight projector that showed the night sky above the house reflected on the nursery ceiling. A state-of-the-art baby monitoring system while they slept alerted them to changes in Morgan's breathing and temperature and allowed them to keep an eye on him from anywhere in the house. Leslie and George suddenly found any excuse to come to visit. And Kennedy's parents had even been thinking about moving to the UK to be closer to their new grandson.

"Hey Mom, no, don't worry, Morgan is sleeping. Hold on, I'll put you on loudspeaker so Jane can hear," Kennedy poked the button and set the phone on the kitchen island.

"Rochelle, Ben, it's so good to hear from you. We miss you already," Jane chimed as she busied herself making lunch.

"Well, you won't have to miss us for much longer," Ben practically sang down the phone.

"Are you coming for another visit?" Kennedy asked.

"Nope. We have bought the house next door; we are moving to England," they cheered down the phone.

When the phone call ended, Kennedy and Jane burst out laughing.

"I know your mother has wanted to move here for years. I just never thought she could convince your dad to do it," Jane laughed.

"She didn't; Morgan did," Kennedy beamed.

A little boy. A ray of light. Morgan was a dream come true, completing the Daniels family and filling the house with even more love. He not only filled a hole in Jane's heart but also brought the entire family closer together. Once divided by an ocean, they would now be right next door.

"How about we have a murder mystery celebration for Morgan's first birthday?" Jane chirped, almost making Kennedy choke on her orange juice.

"I think we have had enough murders around us to last a lifetime. All I want to do now is enjoy being a mom and a wife," Kennedy smiled.

A soft cry emitted through the speakers on the kitchen counter.

"Morgan is awake," Jane grinned.

"Allow me."

The End

Did you enjoy *Jane and Kennedy Daniels Mysteries - Volume 1*?
Please consider rating it on <u>Goodreads</u>, <u>Bookbub</u>, or your favorite retailer. Reviews help me reach new readers.

Read *Jane and Kennedy Daniels Mysteries - Volume 2*

Join my newsletter for writing updates, new releases, recipes, giveaways and promotions!ns!

ABOUT THE AUTHOR

Daisy Landish is a romance and contemporary fiction author whose clean and sweet novellas have tugged at readers' heartstrings around the world. When she's not writing love stories, Daisy spends her time reading, hiking at dawn, and riding into the sunset on her horse, Rosebud.

Join Daisy's Newsletter for updates and giveaways!
www.daisylandishromance.com

facebook.com/daisylandishromance
x.com/daisy_landish
instagram.com/daisylandishbooks
amazon.com/author/daisylandish
bookbub.com/authors/daisy-landish
goodreads.com/Daisy_Landish

ALSO BY DAISY LANDISH

Clean Regency Romance

The Lady Series - The Allington Collection

The Lady Series - The Gillingham Collection

The Lady Series - The Blackmore Collection

The Lady Series - The Norrington Collection

Clean Contemporary Romance

Maplewood Grove Series

Love on Spruce Island

Second Chance

Cherry Tree Island

The Wedding Trio

Extra Credit

Counting on the Cowboy

Focusing on the Cowboy

Mistletoe Magic

Grounded at Christmas

Cozy Mysteries

Sophie Brooks Mysteries

Jane and Kennedy Daniels Mysteries

Pine Grove Mysteries

Annie Archer Paranormal Mysteries

Wilma Wade Holiday Mysteries

Mike and Maddie Mysteries

Mystic Moonhaven Mysteries

Sweater Weather: Cozy Mysteries for Fall

Summer Vibes: Cozy Mysteries for Summer

Let it Snow: Cozy Mysteries for Winter

Spring Break: Cozy Mysteries for Spring